# Moon in Mazatlan

C. L. Kraemer

Published by

**Rogue Phoenix Press**



ISBN 978-1-62420-224-7



Credits

Cover Artist: Designs by Ms G

Editor: Christine Young

## Dedication

To my critique partners A. C. Young and G. Valleau/Genie Gabriel,
thank you for your encouragement.

# One

Corey shifted his bulk from one swollen foot to the other. "I don't know why I couldn't wear my black cowboy boots," he muttered.

"Because you agreed to wear what everyone else is wearing, Corey Williams, or did you leave your memory at home with your badge?" Justin Anderson, dressed in a cream colored tuxedo punched Corey on the shoulder as he walked past his friend.

"When did I agree to that? I don't remember having a vote," Corey turned to Justin and crossed his arms over the cummerbund restraining his waistline.

"You didn't, neither did I nor anyone else. When I asked Diane to marry me, we all lost our votes about wedding stuff. You know, it's a girl thing. We guys go along because the benefits are so great," Justin winked at his friend and smiled as he watched Corey run a finger around the neckline of his tuxedo shirt, pulling it away from his flushed neck.

"This damned thing is choking the life out of me. Why couldn't you guys have waited until winter to get married? Why'd you have to pick the hottest damn day in July? Hell, it's so hot the birds have stopped singing. By the way, how much longer is this going to take?" he growled. He felt sweat trickling down his back as he stood under the shade of the centurion oak tree that graced the town square. The leaves hung limp in the heat of the day.

"I see the girls coming around the corner now. The tall redhead in the light blue is who you'll be escorting down the aisle, but you'd have known that if you'd shown up at the rehearsal," Justin said.

"Justin, I told you I'd be at your wedding if my workload allowed it. To be here today, I had to agree to work two nights for Bob. Oh, wow!"

Corey and Justin stood, mouths gaping, as Justin's bride, Diane, made her way toward the wedding party gathered inside the band gazebo. A cream-colored sheath dress hugged her trim form and the pikake floral headpiece that had been flown in from Hawaii stood out against her dark hair. The sweet fragrance from the headband haloed around Diane. Corey watched his friend's face soften and take on that funny look he'd been wearing since the first time he'd met his fiancée.

*I'd give a month's pay to feel that way about somebody.*

Diane held out her hand and Justin, face beaming, led her to the center of the bandstand wrapping his arms around her tiny waist and gazing into her eyes.

Briana, Justin's daughter, exploded on to the town square, dashing from the church steps over to Corey.

"Uncle Corey! Uncle Corey!"

She ran toward him and jumped, trusting he would catch her.

"Umph!" Corey grunted as the youngster landed in his arms. "You're getting too big for this, young lady." He placed her on the grass where she twirled in front of him and fisted her hands on her developing hips.

"I'm not either. I'm thirteen—not a *young lady*. Besides, Dad says you're stronger than people think and could stop a train if you really wanted. He says you're really, really strong. How'd you like my dress?" Briana twirled in front of Corey again.

"I think you, and your dress, are very beautiful. Look at how tall you are. I'll bet by the end of the year you're taller than me. Then you'll have to catch me." Corey smiled at Briana.

"Hello-o-o-o-o? I need everyone in the wedding party over here, please?" The photographer waved the wedding party to the gazebo, where he manipulated and moved everyone while he took pictures from several angles.

"You boys have ten minutes," the minister's wife tossed over her shoulder as she herded the women to the church. Briana turned and waved at Corey.

"You're one lucky man, Justin," Corey said.

"Yeah, I sure am," Justin smiled, "but it almost didn't happen, remember? If you hadn't been so persistent about following the leads on those sabotaged gas lines at my house, I could've been pushing up daisies right now instead of marrying my soul mate." Justin turned to Corey and shook his hand. "You are a pain in the tukus but a hell of a friend, Corey. Thanks."

Corey's face began to redden. He and Justin usually traded jabs back and forth and he wasn't sure how to handle this compliment.

"Hey, you two, come on! Let's go!"

Tom Manning descended the gazebo steps and, chattering nervously, herded the two tuxedo clad men from the park green to the church entry hall. From the choir loft, strains of music wafted over the pews. The groomsmen ushered guests to their seats and before Corey realized it, the time had come for him to aid his friend Justin in celebrating his wedding day.

He was trying hard not to let the green-eyed monster overcome him. The two had been friends since high school; he knew what kind of living hell Justin had gone through before he'd met Diane. Justin's parents and brother had died in an auto accident, after which Justin's paternal grandmother stepped in and took over care of him and his sister. He'd become bewitched with Ashlee Cline against all his friends' advice. Ashlee had nearly succeeded in killing him but her capture, in the process of trying to flee, sent a collective sigh of relief through the town. The only positive part of his marriage to Ashlee was his daughter Briana. Corey knew Justin deserved every bit of happiness coming his way, but it was hard not to feel envious.

Corey's own life was a shambles after his wife had suddenly decided to *find herself* and divorced him. He'd learned to handle divorced life, but when she took the kids and disappeared, leaving his police contacts spinning their wheels, Corey had tossed in the towel. He quit dating and withdrew. He really was glad his friend Justin had been able to find someone like Diane.

*Who knows? Maybe I will find someone to care for me, someday... yeah, right.*

Tom directed Corey to the center of the entry door. At the pressure of a hand slipping through his crooked elbow, he glanced to his side and found himself escorting the tall curvy redhead to the front of the church. They reached the altar and separated, moving to opposite sides of the minister. Corey kept stealing glances in her direction.

*She's a knockout. Why haven't I noticed her around town before? When and where did Justin meet this woman? Is she a friend of Diane's?* Corey sensed the heat flooding to his cheeks and he blushed crimson when he found himself looking directly into the beauty's eyes. He averted his attention toward the minister marrying his friends, watching as the couple kissed.

"Ladies and gentlemen, I'd like to introduce Justin and Diane Anderson."

The gathered friends and family clapped as several women wiped away tears with tissues. Justin and Diane walked down the aisle to the strains of Billy Idol's "White Wedding" in the background.

"If I may have your attention?" The minister was holding up his hand. "I've been asked to announce that the reception will be held at the new Oakdale Inn on the edge of town. Thank you."

The guests began to gather their belongings.

Corey felt the sweat trickle down his sides, knowing he was going to escort the gorgeous redhead outside. Licking his lips, he turned and offered his arm to her. *She's got dark eyes and she's... stacked. How could I possibly miss this fox in a town this small?*

They stepped into the scorching sunlight, stopping for a moment to catch their breath in the suffocating heat. Corey sensed the hand slip from his arm as he stood blinking in the blinding light. Before his eyes could adjust, the woman had vanished. He ran his finger around his stiffened collar, heat radiating through the opening, and looked around for the statuesque bridesmaid. When he couldn't locate the beauty, he sighed.

*I'd sure like to get out of this monkey suit, but Justin said the photographer wants to take more pictures at the reception.* He clumped down the half dozen steps of the church and lumbered to his truck. *If nothing else, the Inn is air-conditioned. Who in their right mind gets married in July?*

He watched as Justin and Diane drove off in her black Corvette toward the Inn.

Corey limped to his red pickup, the tight rented shoes pinching his swollen feet. The echo of a large motorcycle rumbled through the square and vibrated the air around the truck. He looked around while the guttural rumbling continued to shatter the peace of the small town square.

*The State Police know better than to gun their motorcycles in the center of town. Who the hell is creating so damn much noise?*

Grabbing the handle of his door and placing a swollen foot on the step, he pulled himself into the cab of his truck. A survey of the square, filled with more cars today than usual, and a look down the surrounding streets still didn't reveal the source of the peace-shattering racket. Shrugging, he turned over the engine of the big red truck and slowly navigated the streets. Corey peered into his rear view mirror and frowned. A motorcycle roared past his slow moving vehicle and sped out of the town center. He caught a glimpse of blue chiffon billowing in the breeze and a flash of red hair.

## Two

Corey grabbed for the emergency light and started to accelerate his truck to give chase to the speeding motorcycle. "Nah. Today is my day off. I'll let the boys with the State Police handle this. If I show up late for the reception, Justin and Diane will never let me hear the end of it."

He pulled his foot from the accelerator and cruised to the new Oakdale Inn outside of town. Finding a parking spot close to the entrance and limping slowly, he admired the new hotel. At fifteen stories, it was the tallest building within a twenty-mile radius of the Oakdale and Billington area of Virginia, and had come with a hefty price tag. Justin's construction company had been in the early stages of building the hotel when several explosions rocked the building site, setting fire to equipment and halting the progress. The original investor had been picked up for solicitation of murder charges. Excellent police work, Corey smiled, had turned him on his co-conspirator, Justin's ex-wife, who was trying to have him murdered. When it looked as though the hotel might not be built, the town of Oakdale rallied together and found enough backing to get the project going again. Although the town council argued any building over three stories didn't qualify as an 'inn', they conceded to the name, Oakdale Inn, when their out of town investors agreed not to meddle in town affairs. The provision of one hundred and fifty new jobs helped to ease the argument about the technical definition of an inn. Corey admired the lines of the elegant architecture that created the illusion of age for the new hotel.

He hobbled toward the sliding entry doors. Parked in a no parking zone—bright yellow horizontal lines painted on the ground—next to the front entrance, sat an emerald green Harley Davidson motorcycle with unicorns painted on the gas tank. A quick inspection revealed the engine was still warm. The motorcycle didn't appear to have mechanical troubles. He recalled the flash of blue chiffon and red flying past his truck in town.

*Please, let me be mistaken.* He trudged toward his vehicle. *There are some things I can ignore but blatant disregard of a posted no parking sign is not one of them.*

He retrieved his phone and, with a sigh, called the station.

"Hey, Sarge. It's Corey Williams. Listen, I'm at Justin Anderson's wedding reception here at the Oakdale Inn, and there's some idiot who can't seem to read. Send out a motorcycle tow truck. Yeah, a green Harley Davidson with unicorns on the gas tank parked right in the no parking zone. You'd think the diagonal stripes, No Parking painted on the ground, and the fact no one else was parked there would've clued them. Sure, I'll leave a message at the front desk for them to call you. Thanks, Sarge—What? Oh, yeah, like that's going to happen. If I catch the garter, it's all yours. See ya tomorrow."

Corey replaced his cell in the glove box and once again shuffled his way to the hotel lobby. He unclipped the tie and dropped it into his pocket. He undid the top button on the throat-choking shirt and passed through the sliding entrance doors. The center of the hotel, open to the roof, stopped him in his sweltering tight shoes. Four-story high trees towered over him, and the brook running the length of the hotel reminded him of his favorite hunting spot in the Blue Ridge Mountains.

"Damn." He made his way to the front desk. A clerk he didn't recognize approached.

"Yes, sir. May I help you?" she asked.

"Yes, my name is Corey Williams, Detective Corey Williams. I'm with the Oakdale Police Department." He fished in the pocket of the rented tuxedo and pulled out his badge. "I've called my department to have someone come tow a motorcycle illegally parked out front. If you have a guest who comes in and starts to pitch a fit about their motorcycle being stolen, have them call this number, and we'll handle it from there. Now, can you tell me where the Anderson reception is being held?"

"It's in the Douglas Room just past the Blue Ridge Breakfast Café." The desk clerk pointed down the walkway.

"Thank you, miss."

Corey followed the path beyond the café to enter the Douglas Room, the largest of the reception rooms. The walls were tastefully done in a forest green silk and it featured thick, crème-colored carpet highlighting the floor. Tables with crème linen tablecloths and centerpieces of evergreen boughs, carnations and maroon roses set in crystal bowls, lined the outside of a parquet floor set up in the center for dancing. A bronze plaque on the wall indicated the room capacity was five-hundred people. Corey eyed the crowd inside and wondered what would happen if the Fire Marshall showed up. The entire town of Oakdale appeared to have arrived for the reception. He hadn't seen so many people in one room since the trial of Thomas Manning, Senior. Justin grabbed his arm and steered him to the long table set up at the front of the room. Each place setting included gold-rimmed china with matching gold silverware. Crystal goblets for champagne and water were set in front of each place setting. Corey found himself seated next to the tantalizing redhead.

Justin whispered, "I know how you love redheads. Be careful because Riona handles herself very well." He melted away, reappearing next to his bride.

Corey turned to the goddess residing next to him. "Hello, I'm Corey." He'd stuck out his hand. The redhead surveyed him head to toe. She took his hand in hers and firmly shook it.

"Riona Byrne."

The husky alto reply sent shivers up his back. He opened his mouth to ask a question.

"Attention! Can I have everyone's attention?" Someone at the head table was speaking into a handheld microphone. The room quieted and Tom Manning stood up. "Hello, everyone. Most of you know me but for those who don't, I'm Tom Manning. I've been Justin's best friend since we were kids in grade school."

Everyone shouted, "Hi, Tom," then erupted into laughter.

"To continue..." Tom grinned. "It wasn't too long ago things looked pretty bleak around here. But thankfully, we've all made it through and are here today to celebrate the wedding of Justin and Diane Anderson, two people who, this time last year, were determined not to get married again. Aren't we glad they changed their minds?"

Guests whistled and clapped.

"If you'll all raise your glasses, please." Tom lifted his champagne glass to the newlyweds. "To Justin and Diane… I wish you a lifetime of happiness and whatever success you desire. May you never go to bed angry and may you always find laughter in your lives. Cheers!"

The room was filled with the sound of clinking glasses and applause. Corey turned to the enchantress he'd just met and found himself facing an empty seat. He sighed. *Today is just not my day.*

The call went out for all unmarried men to assemble in the center of the room. Corey struggled out of his chair to join a small group of young boys and grandfathers in the center of the reception room. The wedding garter was removed and tossed to the rowdy group. Absently, he put his hand up and choked when the garter landed in his palm. *Great. Just what I need... the threat of marriage, again.*

He looked to the head table to find Riona smirking at him. The unmarried women were commanded to appear on the floor, and Corey watched closely to see if the enchantress would respond. He smiled to himself. She was easy to spot standing head and shoulders taller than the other women. He easily related to her slightly bored expression. *She doesn't want to spoil this for Justin and Diane any more than I do.*

The center of the room began to bubble with giggles and jostling for position, except for the tall redhead who stood at the back of the group, tightly crossed arms supporting her impressive bust line. The bride turned her back to the rowdy group, and on the shouted count of three threw the bouquet over her head. The crowd rushed forward to capture the prize but it sailed over everyone's head and landed in Riona's folded arms. Corey exploded in laughter at the shocked expression on her face. A camera flash caught the moment. Straightening to her full five foot eleven inches of height, she bowed from the waist and proceeded back to the head table.

"Who the hell came up with these archaic traditions anyway?" she growled as she plopped into the chair.

"I have no clue, but I don't think they're going away anytime soon," Corey said.

"I could live without everyone giving me flak about being single," she said.

"I know what you mean. Everybody has a cousin they're sure you need to meet. Not all of us have a desire to be married," Corey said.

"Boy, have you got that right! I've done damn well without a husband so far, and it doesn't look like I'll be having too many problems in the future requiring one," Riona responded.

"Ladies and gentlemen, may I have your attention please," the DJ announced. "The bride and groom will start this dance alone. On my signal I'd like the wedding party to join them on the floor then the rest of you can come out and dance. Justin? Diane? If you please?"

The newlyweds floated to the center of the floor and began gliding when the music started. They had danced for a few minutes when the DJ asked the rest of the wedding party to join them on the floor.

"I guess that means us." Corey turned to Riona, saying hopefully, "I'll understand if you say no. I haven't danced in nearly ten years. I could do some major damage on your feet."

"No, that's fine. Let's not spoil the day for our friends. Shall we?" Riona nodded to the dance floor.

Corey rose from his chair and moved to help her. He offered his arm and, with Corey limping, they walked on to the dance floor. Tom Manning had taken Justin's daughter as his partner and was twirling her around the floor. Corey turned to Riona and froze. He stood eye to eye with the elegant beauty. *Oh, Lord! I've forgotten how to do this!*

Riona moved into him and, placing one hand on his shoulder, the other in his hand, began to move him around the floor.

"I can't believe I've forgotten how this is done," Corey moaned.

"Don't worry. It's like a bike. You crawl on, kick start the engine, and it will all come back to you," she smiled at him for the first time.

He caught his breath at the difference the smile made on her features. *She is so gorgeous. I'd never stand a chance with her. Those dark eyes and luscious lips are so—so captivating. If I don't stop staring at her, I'll do something stupid like kiss her.*

She turned her head and he noticed the dangling silver earring touching against her shoulders. "Your earrings are very beautiful—unicorns with an emerald?"

"You have a good eye for jewelry. Yes, I had the necklace," she touched her hand to her neck, "and Diane made me a gift of the earrings as thanks for helping her with the wedding."

"They're really beautiful," he said. *The emerald Harley with unicorn tank, unicorn earrings with emerald eyes; I really hope I'm wrong.*

"Thank you. By the way, is there a reason for the limp?" she asked.

"My feet are killing me. My best friend decided to marry on the hottest day of the year and force me to wear these wretched shoes, which don't breathe; hence, my feet are swelling. I don't have any problem when I wear my cowboy boots. Right now, I can't feel my feet. Please tell me I haven't stepped on your toes," he said.

"Nah, you haven't gotten me yet. Listen, I hope you don't mind but I've an early morning appointment and I need to get some beauty sleep. Can we continue this another time?" she asked; the low sexy tones of her voice barely audible over the music.

"Oh, sure. I've a long day tomorrow and should probably think about my own beauty sleep. Shall we?" Corey motioned for her to lead them back to their chairs.

"Finally. I can change to some comfortable clothes," she smiled and moved toward the exit door.

*Man, I'm an idiot. I should have asked if she wanted to have coffee sometime. Boy, did I blow my chances.* Corey grabbed the coffee container on the table and poured himself a cup. *I should go home and get some rest, but I can sleep anytime. It's so great to see Justin and Diane happy. They deserve this.*

He watched his friend dance with his wife. The couple stared dreamily at each other, oblivious to the crowd around them. The music stopped and a comfortable silence settled on the room. Corey watched a tall figure stride cross the empty dance floor. Clad in black leather from boots to headscarf, the figure leaned over and grabbed the microphone from the DJ.

Corey's stomach lurched.

"I need someone to give me a ride to the police station. My Harley's been stolen," the figure removed the glasses and scarf.

Corey groaned when he saw the flash of red hair. *I wish my instincts hadn't been right this time.*

It was Riona Byrne.

## Three

Sighing, Corey struggled to his aching feet. "Miss Byrne? I'm headed to Oakdale. I can drop you at the police station."

Riona handed the DJ his microphone and, her heavy boots thudding against the wooden floor with each step, walked to where Corey was shuffling his weight from swollen foot to swollen foot.

"I really appreciate this. If I ever get my hands on the SOB that stole my Harley, I'll rip him from limb to limb." Her eyes flashed. The beautiful smile had turned to a grim line and the sultry alto voice held an edge.

"I need to say my goodbyes to Justin and Diane. I'll be right back." Corey limped his way to the center of the head table and stood facing a smirking Justin.

"I told you she was capable of handling herself. You didn't have her Harley towed did you, Corey?" Justin started to grin.

"Uh, well, umm, it was parked in a no parking zone," Corey lowered his voice and grimaced.

Justin began to laugh.

"Listen, you guys have a great honeymoon. I gotta go," Corey turned and limped as quickly as he could to Riona. "What say we head to the police station?" he asked.

"Great. The sooner we get there, the sooner the chances of finding my Harley," Riona said.

The two tromped out of the reception through the front lobby.

"Excuse me, Mr. Williams?" The desk clerk was waving at him.

"I think she wants to talk to you," Riona said.

Corey continued to limp as quickly as he could through the sliding front doors into the blast of summer heat. "I'm sure she was talking about someone else." He glanced quickly over his shoulder.

"Yeah, whatever." Riona stood next to the striped pavement. "My Harley was parked right here." She looked at the empty spot then turned to survey the parking lot. With each movement of her head, the silver unicorns on the end of the delicate chains danced in the light.

Corey groaned.

"Are you alright?" Riona asked.

"Just the heat," he said.

"Well, my bike was right here. I can't believe no one saw anything. I mean, how many emerald-colored Harleys are in this town?" Riona glared at the road leading away from the hotel.

"Let's get moving to the police station and initiate your report," he said. *How am I going to tell her I'm the one who had her Harley towed? If I ever had a snowball's chance in hell of taking her out, it just went out the window.* Corey held open the door to the truck.

"I have a truck almost identical to this one at home. It's my winter vehicle, well, was my winter driver. I guess now it will be my all-the-time driver, thanks to some moron," she said.

Corey cringed. *Three hundred seconds to the police station. I'm not sure I'll make it.* He cleared his throat. "Maybe someone made a mistake. Seems to me there's a no parking sign painted on the ground."

"Yeah, and a sign that reads: Motorcycle Parking. I knew this was a small town, but I was sure most people here could read. Enough of them are willing to give me their opinion after every article I write." Riona shifted her helmet on her lap.

The heat and a dark silence in the cab exacerbated the short trip to the station.

Corey guided the truck into a parking space. While the motor was still running and Corey was depressing the parking brake, Riona opened the door and marched inside. Corey watched in stunned silence as his leather clad passenger tromped away from him.

"I'd better get my butt in there before it hits the fan," he muttered. He limped on his swollen feet through the entrance and up to the desk sergeant.

Riona, in the designated waiting area, sat on the edge of the government-issue chair, her helmet held between her knees, tapping a boot clad foot and glaring at the sergeant.

The sergeant broke into a smile when he saw Corey heading toward his desk. Uniformed police began to trickle into the reception room. Catcalls and wolf whistles filled the air.

"Haven't you guys got enough to do? I'm sure I can find several reports needing to be filled out in triplicate for anyone who can't find somewhere else to be." Before the sergeant's threat had left his lips, the room was empty.

"Excuse me, sir, what can I do to help you?" The sergeant pulled a form from a basket in front of him and sat with his pen poised to write.

Corey turned to Riona, "You want to tell this guy what happened?"

Riona strode to the desk. "Yeah, some idiot stole my Harley from in front of the Oakdale Inn. It was parked in the motorcycle zone, and when I came out about ten minutes ago it was gone."

"Is it green with unicorns on the gas tank?" the sergeant asked.

"Yeah! You can't have caught the guy already. I just got here to make the report. How'd you know what it looks like?" Riona was leaning toward the sergeant.

He leaned around her and looked directly at Corey. "Detective?"

Riona whirled around and narrowed her eyes at Corey. "Detective?"

Corey squirmed. *What I wouldn't give to have the earth open up and swallow me right now.* He smiled weakly. "Yeah. I'm Detective Corey Williams. Sarge, can I have the key to the vehicle lock up?"

Limping to the desk and reaching around her, Corey grabbed the keys from the sergeant. Riona stood, arms crossed, helmet dangling from one hand with her feet planted shoulder width. Her emotionless eyes did not betray her thoughts.

He cleared his throat. "If you'll follow me, I think we'll be able to get you on your way."

He limped past the snickering sergeant trying to stifle his amusement behind paperwork. They traveled through the Employees Only door and out to the rear parking area. At the back of the lot, surrounded by a chain link fence, sat a motorcycle and two cars. Riona's step quickened to a trot. She reached the enclosure before Corey and started visually inspecting her bike.

He limped up and, after a couple of false tries, found the correct key for the padlock. He swung open the gate and leaned against it as Riona pushed past him to her bike. She knelt down and ran her hands over every inch of the machine.

"You were parked in a no parking zone," Corey started feebly.

Riona stopped. She looked up at him and shook her head. "There was a posted *motorcycle parking* sign. I'm not so arrogant to think I can park my bike just anywhere. I'll go take a picture of the damned thing if that will make you happy."

"Uh, that's not necessary. Listen, this is just a misunderstanding. Why don't you get your bike out and we'll just forget this happened?"

"Sure. There doesn't appear to be any damage, and I need to get home. Tomorrow is going to be hectic." Riona rose and stored her stuff in the saddlebags on the side of the motorcycle. She ran her hand through her hair then donned her helmet. Swinging one long leg over the gas tank, she sat on the deep emerald leather seat to adjust the mirrors then stood and kick started the bike. Twisting the gas handle with one hand and holding the clutch with the other, she gunned the motor. The low, guttural growl of the engine echoed off the buildings and rattled the windows of the station. Toeing the clutch into gear, she slowly gave the engine gas and the wheels began to move.

"Listen, Riona, I'm really sorry..." Corey started. His voice disappeared in the potato-potato-potato sound of the engine as the motorcycle cleared the gate and moved into the parking area. Once free of the chain link enclosure, Riona gunned the engine and roared out of the parking lot.

Corey sighed as he relocked the gate. *I was sure there wasn't any parking allowed there. Man, what a screw up.*

He trudged back to the station, past the smirking desk sergeant and out to his truck. He had a conference with the District Attorney tomorrow and, right now, the only thing he wanted to do was take off these cursed shoes and soak his feet in hot water and Epson salts. Now, if he could just get the leather-clad redhead off his mind, he'd be batting a thousand. *Fat chance.*

# Four

Riona roared out of the parking lot and immediately slowed to the speed limit. *All I need now is a speeding ticket. Better safe than sorry, and broke.*

The state law didn't require helmets for riding, but she'd covered too many accidents where motorcyclists had tangled with moving vehicles or trees and lost. Because they weren't wearing helmets, they'd lost permanently. Besides that, a helmet disguised her gender, and she got less hassle from other drivers. The half hour ride to Billington was an enjoyment most of the time, but today she, like Corey, had been shoved into a situation and clothes she didn't like. Her feet hurt in her riding boots and the soaring temperature was making her leathers stick to her skin. *A cool shower and cotton shorts will feel so good. It's really too bad Corey's a cop. He's kind of cute...and shy. You sure don't find that very often.*

She slowed as she entered the city limits of Billington. Driving through the center of town, she surveyed the summer tourists clogging the streets. Her emerald Harley drew few looks from the out-of-towners who drove in from the surrounding areas to shop in the antique malls that dotted the community. Riona turned down the second street north of the town center. A mile drive brought her to the turn, leading to a ranch style home she had purchased from the original owner, where a quarter mile drive up the narrow tree lined lane ended at her garage. She slowly drove the motorcycle inside, planted her feet on the ground and automatically closed the garage door. Humming an unidentifiable tune, she kicked the stand to the ground and let the motorcycle rest on it. She removed the helmet and ran her leather free fingertips through her cropped red hair. She retrieved the crumpled bridesmaid outfit and crushed bouquet from the saddlebags and exited out the side door. Before she realized it, she was standing in front of the dog run.

"Oh, Kumari. I miss you so much." Riona's fingers gripped the chain link and a tear slid down her sunburned cheek. Immediately after her interview with Justin Anderson had been published in the Billington and Oakdale papers, her beloved Ridgeback dog was poisoned. Riona wiped angrily at another tear coursing down her cheek. *Enough self-pity.*

Turning on a booted heel, she moved into the house and her bedroom. She peeled the leather from her body and, closing her eyes, reveled in the cool breeze from the air conditioner gently swirling around her. Shedding her remaining clothes, she padded to the shower. As the cool water sluiced down her body, her mind wandered back to her escort of the afternoon.

"He's kind of cute in a cuddly teddy bear way, but he's a cop," Riona's voice echoed back to her. "And a small town cop at that. He had my motorcycle towed, damn it, and I'm sure he was wrong about the no parking sign. I know I saw a sign for motorcycle parking. But what if he's right? God, I'd have to apologize—or would I? Arghh! I'll work this out later."

She towel dried and changed into clean shorts and a tank top. Riona was beginning to feel like herself again. She had an assignment needing more research, so she wandered to the room that served as her office and flipped on the police scanner before sitting at her computer.

Tapping in the newspaper's password, she logged on to The Billington Bulletin's website and searched the back issues for stories about her latest subject. A summons for her to receive the only interview given by Ashlee Anderson, currently in jail for the attempted murder of Justin Anderson, her ex-husband, landed in Riona's in-box less than a week ago. Riona hadn't said anything to Justin and Diane because it was their wedding day. Their sworn statements had released them from appearing in court, and they were free to enjoy the beginning of their new life together.

Ashlee Cline Anderson had been accused of trying to arrange the murder of her ex-husband to collect monies he was leaving to their daughter, Briana. The story around town was Ashlee had coerced her live-in boyfriend and another long-time lover into helping her arrange for the murder. But Riona felt there was more happening than the police were releasing to the press. *That's it! I knew Corey's name was familiar. He was the lead detective on this case. Hmmm. Maybe I should apologize after all. It can't hurt to have someone on the inside.* Riona grinned. *I am devious.*

She typed Corey's name into the search engine at the paper's website and sat back in her chair to wait. A few seconds later the headline: SABOTAGE IN BLUE MOUNTAIN COMMUNITY jumped at her from the monitor screen.

"Oh, yeah, Bill Johnson had the lead on this story but I was there. I wonder why I don't remember Corey. He must have been in the background or I would've recalled a good looking man like him."

The police scanner crackled and Riona leaned over to turn up the volume. It turned out to be Winifred Miller's usual Saturday night call to have someone climb up the 100 year old oak tree in her front yard and rescue her cat, Tomboy. Riona turned the volume lower as she continued to research the archives. The slant Bill Johnson had put on the subsequent stories made Riona's reporting nerves cringe. It was evident the reporter had lost no love for Ashlee Anderson, and several of his statements were borderline slander, but no one had complained to the paper, including Ashlee Anderson's family.

"I am amazed these people haven't taken Bill to court. Makes me wonder, why not? Are they going to appeal this case and cite Bill's biased reporting? This should prove to be an interesting interview."

She stifled a yawn and stretched her sore muscles. Standing in high heels for the wedding and reception had cramped her legs enough that even the shower hadn't stopped the throbbing. Getting up from her desk and closing her office, Riona gravitated to the bathroom.

*I'll take some aspirin and go to bed. Maybe that will stop these muscles from aching.* She stood in front of the medicine cabinet, absently staring at the reflection in the mirror. *I want to watch her work. Any woman who can get two men to try to murder a third man is someone who needs watching. I feel a really big story here. I just need to be sharp enough to recognize it.*

~ * ~

Ashlee Cline Anderson sat behind the double pained bulletproof glass, eyeing the dark haired young man in a business suit shuffling through his briefcase on the opposite side. *Another new lawyer, great. I wonder how many weeks ago he passed the Bar?*

She tapped on the glass and pointed to the phone on the wall. They picked up simultaneously and Ashlee widened her eyes innocently as she asked, "Who are you, and where is my lawyer, Debbie?"

"I—I'm Gerald Ingram, and I'll be representing you. Deborah, uhm, took a job with a private law firm." Gerald fingered the gold latches on his dark brown briefcase.

Ashlee pushed her lower lip into a seductive pout. "I don't want another lawyer. Now I have to tell my story all over again." Tears began pooling in her eyes and her lower lip started to quiver.

"No, no! I know I've got your file in my briefcase here somewhere." Gerald put down the phone on the stained counter and rummaged through the case, triumphantly pulling out a yellow file folder bulging with papers. He grabbed the receiver and announced, "See? I told you it was here. No, Deborah briefed me very thoroughly when she assigned the case to me. I think we might be able to get these charges dismissed for lack of evidence. I promise; you won't go to jail." Gerald leaned toward the glass, his brow slightly furrowed, his intense brown eyes holding Ashlee's ice blue ones in his gaze.

"But I'm already in jail," she said softly, allowing a tear to streak down her cheek.

"I—I know but I can't change that. The judge feels like you're a flight risk. He won't budge on letting you out on your own recognizance. I—I'm truly sorry." Gerald slipped the file folder back into the briefcase.

Ashlee sighed and slid back in the chair, stretching the line of the phone to its maximum. "I guess there's nothing you can do. Is my interview tomorrow morning still on?"

"Oh, yes. Ms. Byrne has agreed to submit her questions before we get started and abide by our decisions." Gerald glanced at his watch. "Listen, I'm sorry but I have another appointment I need to keep. I just wanted to introduce myself, and let you know I was handling your case. Well, I'll see you tomorrow morning, Ms. Anderson. Until then."

He hung up the phone and, snatching his briefcase, quickly exited the visiting area. Ashlee watched her new lawyer escape. *He's perfect. He'll play right into my plans.*

She lit a cigarette and blew smoke rings into the air. Tomorrow, she'd lay down the first phase of her plan. March in Mazatlán—she could smell the honeysuckle and feel the sun on her face.

~ * ~

Riona stopped and took her aspirin, then walked to the door of her bedroom. She reached in to turn on the light, her skin rippling with goose bumps as she shivered from a sudden icy draft enveloping her body. She jerked around to look down the hallway, expecting to see someone standing at the end, but it was empty. The icy draft snaked up her back and, as quickly as it had grabbed at her, it disappeared.

Riona flipped the overhead light on and moved to the nightstand by her bed. She changed into her sleeping shirt and flipped off the overhead. Tonight, she would leave the nightstand light on—just tonight.

## Five

Corey sat at his large desk pushing paperwork from one side to the other. The memory of the redhead swinging her leg over the motorcycle and kick starting the green monster still lingered. He broke into a sweat at the thought of a woman, that woman, handling the Harley with such ease.

*If she can handle that much machine so easily, imagine what she can do with a man.* He stared into space allowing his mind to wander. *I have got to stop thinking about her. This trial needs my undivided attention. Aside from that, having her motorcycle towed blew any chance I had of getting to know her better.* His reverie was broken by the buzz of his intercom.

"Yes, Sarge?"

"The District Attorney is here to see you, Corey."

"Send him back."

Shifting his chair forward and stacking his unfinished paperwork, he cleaned the top of his desk until Elias McCafferty, County District Attorney, poked his head around Corey's door.

"Hey, Corey."

"Hey, Elias. Come in and sit down. You want a cup of coffee?" Corey said.

A gangly silver haired man ambled through the door and plunked himself into the chair facing Corey.

"Nah, I've spent the last hour sitting over at Sallianne's Coffee Shop talking with Billy Somes about where we might be going deer hunting this year. We've pretty well hunted out our normal spot, and Billy thinks he might want to go a little farther north. I guess it just depends whether his wife visits her mother or stays in town. You know how that goes." Elias winked at Corey.

"Yeah, maybe if I had gone hunting farther north I might still be married. Guess I'll never know. How's our case looking for trial next week?" Corey said.

"That's why I wanted to meet with you. I have a gut feeling we're overlooking something." Elias flipped the end of his tie with his fingers as he crossed and uncrossed his long thin legs.

"Elias, would you stop worrying? The judge signed the warrants. The evidence we had, and still have, is irrefutable and safely under lock and key. I'll bet my life on it. I can have one of the officers pull the files if you want to go over them one more time," Corey said.

"No. I just have this gut feeling the defense is planning some sort of ambush in court. There's been no communication from their office to mine. Usually in a case this messy I'll get at least one phone call trying to work a deal, but I've heard nothing from the Public Defender's Office. I'd have thought the inflammatory articles written in the Billington Bulletin would've raised some ruckus. If it had been a client of mine, I'd have been screaming bloody murder." The attorney fidgeted in his seat.

"We have solid evidence of who was involved, and a recording, and back-up, of the request for a murder to be committed, plus the transaction of money exchange as well as the money. Why don't you give me an idea of your prosecution plan? I can clear up small points and show you where you might be weak when it comes to the evidence. Outside of that, Elias, it's really out of our hands. You need to trust our judicial system. I'll make a bet if the jury pool is chosen from the people in the county; there'll be half of them with a dislike for Mr. Manning or Ashlee Anderson. Those two have cut a wide swath of destruction," Corey said.

"Well, you're probably right about that. Not too many people I've talked to feel any real sympathy for either of them. Let's review the case just one more time." Elias scooted his chair to the desk and, snapping his briefcase open, he pulled out papers which he spread over the top of Corey's desk. When the DA felt confident of his presentation, he gathered the papers into his briefcase and moved to the door.

"Thanks, Corey. I think we've got them on this one. I'm going to recommend Ashlee be sent away for the maximum years possible. I just wish I could do the same for Mr. Manning. It irritates me he's a lawyer; gives the rest of us a bad name. I'll see you in court next Monday." Elias departed; a smug look on his face.

"In my opinion, all lawyers have a bad name," Corey muttered softly as he smiled and waved at Elias. "But if he can get Ashlee put away, I'm all for that."

Prior to Elias's visit, Corey hadn't worried about the upcoming trial. He had audio recordings of the final murder-for-hire meeting, and two co-defendants who were willing to testify against Ashlee to save their own hides. While Elias had walked out the door with his doubts assuaged, Corey was beginning to feel naggings of his own.

Early in the investigation, Corey had secured Ashlee's college transcripts and learned she had been a pre-law major who had graduated in the top two percent of her college class.

He'd seen through her poor-pitiful-me act early in his friend, Justin's, marriage and made numerous excuses bowing out of invitations because of Ashlee. She was intelligent, and money hungry. Corey hadn't been the only person glad to see Justin divorce the woman. However, even with the knowledge of her duplicity, Corey had not been able to solve the question of how Ashlee had escaped being picked up with Thomas Manning, Sr.

According to Mr. Manning Sr., after meeting with the man they thought was a hit man, Ashlee had been highly aroused and begged to leave the restaurant so they could make love at his cabin in the country. She'd never shown up and wasn't present when the police arrived to arrest him.

"There is no way she could've known about the arrest," Corey said. "It irritates me she disappeared so conveniently and now, this woman who has temper tantrums when the cleaners press her slacks the wrong way is being conspicuously quiet. I don't like it. I don't like it at all."

Corey rose from his desk and began pacing the length of his office. He chewed the end of a pencil as he walked. When his phone rang, he spit pieces of eraser out of his mouth before answering.

"Yes?"

"Corey, this is Elaine Madison in the woman's section of the jail. You wanted me to contact you if I came across anything unusual regarding Ms. Anderson," she said.

"Yes, Elaine, what is it?" Corey asked.

"Well, she's giving an interview to the Billington Bulletin tomorrow at ten o'clock. I have a…umm, let's see, here it is, reporter Riona Byrne authorized to interview. Seems Ms. Anderson won't speak with anyone else. Do you want me to do anything about it?" Elaine asked.

Corey sighed. "No, Elaine, you've done as I asked, thank you."

The mention of Riona's name conjured a picture of the statuesque goddess in Corey's mind.

"You'll be the death of me yet, Riona," he muttered. He needed to see that interview before it was published. *How the hell am I gonna do that? She's not likely to hand it over after today. I've got less than twenty-four hours to come up with a plan.*

He sat and tapped his finger against his forehead. His eyes lit up and he slapped his hand on the desk. "I've got it!" Picking up the phone, he dialed Elias's number. "Hello, Elias? How soon can I get a court order to get the phones in the jail bugged?"

"What do you need it for?" Elias answered.

"Ashlee Anderson is giving an interview tomorrow, and I want to know what's said before the newspaper reporter cuts and edits everything. Maybe she'll get cocky and give something away," he said.

"Well, Corey, we've had the phones in the jail tapped for about two years now. Where've you been?"

What do you mean?" he growled.

"Corey, it's a precaution we started when the Billington Police Department started getting threats. Most interrogation rooms all over the country have recording devices and cameras. I thought you knew," Elias said.

"Well, I didn't. We don't get much real crime in our small town, thank God, so this is the first felony I've worked on in several years. Okay, who do I talk to about getting the tapes?"

"I believe the desk sergeant keeps track of the tapes and is supposed to file them daily. Check with him. Now if you don't mind, I have a client." Elias hung up.

"Learn something new every day," Corey muttered to himself. "At least, I'll get to hear the interview before it goes to print. I wonder if Ashlee will try to work Riona like she does everyone else."

Corey headed down the hallway to the soda machine.

"Hey, Corey! Where's your tux?" The younger officers hadn't let up on him since he'd stopped after the wedding to release Riona's motorcycle.

"You're not special enough." Corey wasn't going to let the ribbing spoil his day. He'd apologize profusely to Riona, right before asking her to go out for coffee. His stomach fluttered, and he cleared the dusty feeling from his throat with a swig of soda.

Gazing out the break room window, he ruminated.

*If I don't blow this, too, I'll have a date for the first time in five years. I wonder if I still know how to act on a date? Guess we'll find out if Riona says yes. If she says no… back to square one.*

Corey tilted the soda up and finished the contents. He dropped the empty can into the recycling bin and trudged back to his office. He still had paperwork to prepare for the trial. The thought made his stomach roll sourly. A nasty suspicion in the back of his head nagged at him; Ashlee Anderson wasn't content to sit in jail quietly. As Corey entered his office, a chill raced up his spine.

"I don't like this. Hopefully, by this time next month, Ms. Ashlee will be the problem of the state. I just wish I could get rid of this feeling of dread," he said. Moving to the window air conditioner, he checked the setting. The chill had burrowed its way into his spine.

"This is nonsense. I've got too much paperwork to give in to ominous feelings. I'm sure Ashlee will be convicted and sent to prison, and Oakdale will get back to being its normal quiet self. Now where is that vehicle report form I filled out on Riona's motorcycle?"

The small voice continued to nag at him that something was not right. He pushed it away and buried himself in reports.

Corey jumped when the phone rang. "What?" he barked.

"Detective Williams? This is patrolman Kurt Lee. Ashlee's mom asked me to take a letter to her. I know you're screening her visitors and mail and wanted to check in with you first. Will there be a problem?"

"No, but Lee?"

"Yes, sir."

"Why did they ask you to bring the letter in?" Corey's brow furrowed as he waited for the answer.

"Ashlee's mom and my aunt have been best friends since grade school. They both live in Winchester and the last time I visited my aunt she volunteered me to act as mail carrier. Is it okay?" Kurt asked.

The silence on the phone stretched as Corey thought. "Yeah, go ahead. Just make sure the matron reads the mail first, you understand?" he asked.

"Yes, sir. Thank you, detective."

"No problem."

He spied the paperwork he'd been searching for and, carefully separating the copies, ran them through the shredder next to his desk. The corners of his mouth curled up and he softly whistled. There would be no record of the tow.

*How can she be mad at me now? I think I'll go to lunch. I've had a busy morning.*

The chill fingered his spine one more time as he got up to leave. Corey spun around and reached for the controls of the air conditioner. *It's off. I've already turned it off. What the hell is going on*?

Grabbing his black cowboy hat, Corey fled the room. *I'm just hungry, that's all. As soon as I eat, all this foolishness will vanish.*

He pushed open the doors to exit the station and was assaulted with a wave of heat. He immediately broke in to a sweat. *What a weird day.*

He turned at the bottom of the steps and headed to Sallianne's Coffee Shop. There was nothing a Sallianne Burger Bust couldn't cure. Corey licked his lips in anticipation. The next hour was for eating. Everything else could just wait.

## Six

Patrolman Kurt Lee walked to the women's section of the jail and knocked on the glass window of the duty room. Matron Elaine Madison looked up and pushed the button under her desktop. The door buzzed and Kurt heard the click of the lock disengaging. The distinctive musty smell of government institution assaulted his nose. He wrinkled it as he pushed open the door and stepped into the duty office.

"Elaine, how are you?" he said.

"Fine, Kurt. What's wrong?"

"How do you put up with the smell?" He grimaced.

"You get used to it. Every jail I've worked in has that musty dusty smell. What are you doing in my section of the world?" She raised her eyebrows in question.

"My aunt committed me to being her delivery boy. I've got a letter for Ashlee Anderson I need to leave with you. Can you see she gets it? I'll be in deep trouble if she doesn't. Besides, my aunt is my only relative with money. Don't want to screw up my chances at inheriting, know what I mean?" Kurt winked as he placed the envelope on the desk.

"Sure, Kurt, you can buy me dinner when you get rich." Elaine picked up the envelope and ripped open the top, pulling a page from inside. Kurt waved as he left the office and waited while Elaine buzzed him out, waving again as he disappeared down the hallway.

"Let's see what we have here," Elaine opened the single page and read.

> *Dear Ashlee,*
>
> *I hope you're doing well. I wish you would call and let me speak with you. As I said in my other letters, I couldn't say anything with the police standing in the living room next to me. They were watching me very closely. That being said, I thought I'd let you know that your daughter, Briana, is doing well. Everything Has Been Planned And Is A Go for her to attend school next year while she lives with Justin and his new wife, Diane.*
>
> *I wanted to be sure you didn't worry about her. Please call me, and let me know they're treating you well.*
>
> *Love, Mom*

Elaine chuckled, "I'm sure Ashlee really wants to hear about Justin being happy. This should keep her quiet all night long. No whining about how she doesn't deserve to be here and bragging about everything she's going to get when she gets out of here. It might actually be a pleasant evening."

She left the office and, unlocking the outer gate, moved to the cell where Ashlee Anderson was spending her time.

"Mail call. A letter for you, Ms. Anderson," she said handing the envelope through the bars.

"This has been opened." Ashlee glared directly into the blue eyes of the matron.

"Like everything else that comes to you, all your mail and visitors will be screened until you leave our lovely resort," Elaine answered.

"If you don't mind, I'd like to read this in private." Ashlee snatched the letter from the blonde jailer's hand and moved to the bunk.

"Sure." Elaine grinned as she glanced at the camera. *Fat chance honey. Everything in your life is public viewing. Better get used to it cause it isn't gonna change when you go to prison.*

Elaine, whistling tunelessly, walked back to the office.

Ashlee yanked out the plain sheet of paper and quickly scanned the contents until the one line she was anticipating stopped her. She smiled and let the letter flutter to the bunk as she leaned against the cell wall. *This time next week, you fat slug, I'll be laying on the beach in Mazatlán sipping drinks with little umbrellas in them.*

She steepled her fingers under her chin; *now I have got to find a way around the female reporter from the Bulletin. She seems hardened, and I don't think she'll fall for my poor pitiful little girl schtick. Maybe, I can appeal to her feminist side. I've only got twelve hours to make this work for me.*

Ashlee lay on her bunk, hands tucked behind her head, formulating a plan to use for the next day's interview. She'd always been able to get people to come around to her side of any issue. This time, her freedom was at stake. She needed to gather some sympathy from the community. It appeared her lawyer wasn't going to ask for a change of venue so she needed to come off as another victim of Thomas Manning, Sr.

She licked her lips and slowly smiled. *I can do this.*

The lights flickered and a disembodied voice announced: "Ten o'clock. Lights out."

Ashlee continued to smile. *Mazatlán. I can't wait.*

## Seven

Riona groaned as the alarm buzzed loudly. *I hate interviews where I have to submit my questions first. It damn near gags any real information from the interviewee, but, I guess that's the defense's point.*

She swung her legs over the edge of the bed and slipped her feet into flip-flops while slipping her arms through a sleeveless cotton wrap. Slap, slapping down the hallway to her office, she grumbled and rubbed the sleep out of her eyes. She'd awakened at one o'clock in the morning and written the questions she'd planned to ask. She'd e-mailed them to the lawyer's office as requested, and now all she needed was the approval to use them.

She sat down and flipped on the computer, watching the screen flicker and fade to blue. When she finally opened her email, she found the attorneys had nixed half her questions.

"Crap. I don't need to try and think this damned early in the day. I'm not doing anything until I've had coffee and taken a shower." Riona flipped the computer off and trudged to the kitchen.

One bagel and two cups of coffee later, she sat down to the computer and sent in her questions for approval, typing: "I will ask your client to tell her side of the story, without direct questions, and you can approve or nix the story as we go along." *There.*

Riona sat back in the chair and gloated at the light blue screen. *I suspect allowing your client to talk freely will get me more answers than any questions I could have asked. My research tells me this Anderson woman does NOT like to lose control of any situation and sitting in jail probably doesn't suit her very well. Let's see you control her now.*

Shutting down the computer and moving toward the bathroom, Riona was stopped in the middle of the hallway by a stream of ice-cold air raising the hair on her arms. She shivered and whipped around to look behind her.

"This is ridiculous. It's just my imagination." She quickly finished her morning routine and moved toward the office after forty-five minutes. Today, she'd chosen to wear tailored khaki pants with a subtly printed silk blouse that accented her chocolate brown eyes.

She opted to drive the pickup instead of ride her Harley. Her background research had shown her Ashlee Anderson used intimidation to gain the upper hand in everything. Arriving crisp, despite the heat, and moving with the assurance of an experienced reporter, Riona could control the direction of the interview.

She checked in with the desk sergeant and was escorted into the visitor's area, where a man in an off-the-rack brown business suit moved toward her.

"Ms. Byrne?" The young man extended his hand. "I'm Gerald Ingram, and I'm representing Ashlee Anderson in her proceedings. I received your e-mail this morning and, while I can't argue with your approach, I don't see how this interview will be worthwhile to you. However, if you feel you want to continue, I'll be more than happy to have the matron bring Ms. Anderson to the visiting area."

Riona noticed Gerald shifting from foot to foot and switching his briefcase back and forth. The corners of her mouth turned slightly. *This is his first case, and he got dumped with the hottest happening in the county. He's probably soaked under his suit jacket.*

"Mr. Ingram, I can abide by the rules you've laid down. Shall we have Ms. Anderson join us?" She smiled and nodded in the direction of the two chairs set on one side of bulletproof glass. The reporter and lawyer took their places. The jail door opened and Ashlee Anderson came through the opening in a county issued orange jumpsuit. She thanked the jailer who handed her a pack of cigarettes and matches. Ashlee smiled weakly at the pair seated in the visitation booth. Slumping into the chair, she brushed a stray hair away from her face and raised her lackluster eyes to meet her attorney's gaze.

"God, she looks like hell. What the devil happened last night? When I left she seemed to be in fairly good spirits," Gerald commented to Riona.

The trio picked up the phones and Gerald started.

"What happened last night, Ashlee? You seemed to be doing alright, what changed?" he said.

Ashlee sighed. "I just got a letter from my mom. I really miss her and my daughter, that's all. It's hard to sleep in here at night with all the noise, so I just toss and turn. I'm sorry. I guess I must look a sight. Once you get me off, Mr. Ingram, I can go back to my mother's and things will be alright." She had slowly straightened herself in the chair and was beaming at Gerald Ingram.

Riona stared. *My God, what a manipulator. I can see why the women in this town turn their noses up and sniff when asked about Ashlee Anderson.*

Gerald Ingram turned to Riona.

"I'll allow her to tell her story as long as it doesn't impinge on the case I've prepared for trial. If I feel it strays in to that area or might incriminate my client, I'll direct her to refuse to answer. Are we clear?" Gerald asked.

"I'm clear, Mr. Ingram. It's nice to meet you, Ms. Anderson. I think I can make this simple. I would like to hear your side of the story. I checked all of the papers in the area and found no one had talked with you to find out what you had to say. I'd like it if you would tell me, in your own words, what happened. How did you wind up in jail for this alleged crime?"

Riona watched the face of the woman across from her relax into a smooth alabaster mask. Ashlee pulled a cigarette from the pack on the shared counter. She lit it and, inhaling deeply, gazed thoughtfully at Riona.

"So you want to hear my side of the story?"

Riona nodded. Her pen was poised over her notepad.

"Why?"

Riona looked at Gerald who nodded his approval.

"There's no record of anyone talking with you. It's been almost a year since the alleged incident took place and I can't find one, not one story, where the press asked what was happening with you at the time. To me it seems one sided, as well as poor reporting. I know you have a perfectly good explanation. I'd like to be the reporter who gets the story. That's all."

Ashlee blew a long stream of smoke at the glass partition. She searched Riona's face, stopping at the dark brown eyes. Snubbing out the cigarette, she leaned forward toward the glass and took a deep breath. "All right, but I want to see the copy before it goes to press or I'll veto the article." Ashlee thumped her forefinger on the glass.

Riona jumped when the glass rattled. *Isn't she the smart one? I'm not sure I want her to tell me how to write this article. I'm going to call her bluff.*

"Well, I guess I'd better get going then. I don't allow anyone to tell me how to write. I felt you might have something to say that would quiet your detractors, but I won't give up my right to present this story my way. I'm sorry to have wasted your time, Ms. Anderson, Mr. Ingram." Riona hung the phone up and rose from her chair, picking up her notepad and purse. She heard furious tapping on the glass.

"Miss Byrne, please."

The look on Gerald Ingram's face caused Riona to hesitate.

"Please. We'll give up the right to read the copy before printing. Ms. Anderson would like to have her side of the story revealed."

Riona placed her pad on the counter and looked at the woman on the other side. Ashlee's face was flushed. She mouthed *please*. Riona sat in the chair and put the phone to her ear.

"All right, but you have to trust me. I'm a reporter who wants a story no one else has gotten. Judgment is for judges and juries, not good reporters. Do we have an agreement?"

Ashlee nodded and lowered her head.

"Tell me your story."

The sigh was audible at Riona's end of the phone. She looked at the form slumped in the chair and her heart began to soften. The orange jumpsuit swallowed the tiny brunette whose head hung down. When Ashlee looked up, tears pooled in the ice blue eyes and her lower lip quivered slightly. Sighing deeply, she straightened herself in the chair and brushed her hand at the unshed tears and began to speak.

"About a year ago, I was living with a man named Paul. Unfortunately, things were not going well and I turned to a family friend for advice. On top of everything else happening to me; my ex-husband began giving me problems about paying child support for our daughter." A sob escaped and Ashlee buried her face in her hands. Her shoulders shook slightly for a moment, and she gulped several deep breaths of air then continued.

"I foolishly made the comment to both my friend and my lover that life would be so much easier if my ex-husband were permanently out of the picture. I mean, everybody says things like that when they're frustrated. I didn't mean for anybody to do anything about it. Well, apparently, both guys took me seriously and decided to make my wish come true. The next thing I know, I hear the gas lines have been disabled at Justin's house and explosives have been rigged at his work site. I was flabbergasted anything like this would happen here in Oakdale. So I called my friend to find out what the story was. Paul, my boyfriend, had started having a fling with someone else while still living under my roof." Ashlee sat straight in the chair clenching her fists on the counter, her face flushed with righteous anger.

"He moved out after the broadcasts featuring the police at my ex's house. Some of the things he left behind made me think he'd been directly involved. I was afraid for my daughter and myself. After all, this man had been living in our house. Who knows what could have happened?"

Ashlee stopped and wiped at nonexistent tears with one hand as she reached for a cigarette. She lit it and took a deep drag, blowing a lazy stream of smoke toward the ceiling.

"I contacted my friend, and we made a date to have dinner and discuss the items I'd found in the house. I knew he'd be able to tell me what to do. He said he had to meet with some business associates at the restaurant before we ate, but it wouldn't take long then he'd be able to devote the rest of the evening to helping me solve my problem. We met the men, and they talked while I sat waiting for my friend. I wasn't paying attention to them. I couldn't tell you, to this day, any of the conversation, but somehow the police came to the conclusion I was planning to murder my ex-husband!"

At this point, Gerald cleared his throat and spoke up. "I think we're getting into dangerous territory here, Ms. Anderson."

Ashlee narrowed her eyes. "She asked to hear my story, and this is part of it."

"I know, uhm, Ms. Anderson, but I don't want to, ah, jeopardize our case. Maybe we should call it a day and Miss Byrne can work with what she has so far."

Ashlee leaned back in her chair and blew smoke rings for a minute. She punched out the cigarette and leaned toward the glass.

"I want to tell my story, *all* of my story. It's not fair no one has heard my side."

Riona watched the woman. Her eyebrows knit together in concern and her eyes began to pool with tears. A single tear trickled down the alabaster cheek. The mouth turned down at the edges and her bottom lip began to protrude and quiver. *She's really working this guy.*

Gerald leaned toward the glass, unconsciously placing his hand against the clear divider. "Please, Ashlee, don't cry. I—I didn't realize telling your side of the story meant that much to you. Please continue, we'll pick up the pieces later."

Ashlee sucked in a ragged breath and cleared her throat. "To finish," she delicately wiped a tear from her eye, "having my ex-husband killed would have been the stupidest thing I could do. He was still providing the majority of my income. Personally, I think my ex-boyfriend decided to get even with me. I'd promised him money if he helped with a few renovations on the house where my daughter and I were living. When I refused to pay him the final installment because of poor workmanship, he decided to get back at me. That's the only thing that would tie me to any of this foolishness. All these other stories are just that—stories. I'm quite sure Mr. Ingram will clear this up and, by next month, I'll be home with my daughter."

Riona opened her mouth to correct Ashlee, but the warning look in Gerald Ingram's eyes silenced her.

"Well, Ms. Anderson, I thank you for your time. I'll take what I have and if I get the final piece written before deadline, I'll send a copy to Mr. Ingram for his perusal." Riona hung up the phone and, shaking hands with the attorney, left the visitor area. Looking up into the large fisheye mirror, she saw the attorney and client leaning toward each other deep in conversation.

~ * ~

"Mr. Ingram," Ashlee started.

"Gerald," he corrected.

"Gerald, how much corra—corroborating evidence do they have to tie me to this?" Ashlee leaned toward the glass, flashing her ample cleavage at her lawyer and shyly batting her black lashes.

"Uh, well, they say they have a paper trail that connects you with the two other defendants," Gerald started.

"That's crap," Ashlee muttered.

"What?"

"I said it was a trap," Ashlee widened her eyes.

"Well, uh, uh, they do have the testimony of the other two defendants implicating you and, while Mr. Zachary has been a felon, Mr. Manning is a well-known member of the Bar. His testimony will be carefully measured and considered accurate by most people. I'll do everything in my power to get you off, but I can't make any guarantees."

Ashlee leaned back in the institutional chair.

"Then, what you're telling me is you're giving up before the trial has even started?"

"Uh, no, Ms. Anderson, I'm just making you aware the prosecution has a very strong case against you. Any, I repeat, any hard evidence you might have to repudiate their claims will be greatly appreciated. I prefer to win my cases," Gerald said.

"Gerald? I can't-do-hard-time. I'll rehash everything that happened to see if I may have missed anything, but I can't do time for a crime I didn't commit. Please tell me you'll get me out of here." Ashlee scooted to the edge of the chair. She furrowed her brow and her ice blue eyes darkened to deep gray. Her face clouded, and Gerald noticed her breasts raising and lowering rapidly.

"Ms. Anderson, please don't work yourself into a state. We'll handle this, please..." Gerald trailed off as he watched the young woman's eyes roll back into her head, and she slumped forward. He jumped from his chair when her body fell toward the counter edge. He slammed his hands against the reinforced glass as he helplessly watched Ashlee's forehead meet with the counter edge, split, and begin to bleed.

Gerald yelled and banged on the glass. The matron appeared and, seeing Ashlee, opened the door and uttered an expletive when she saw the widening puddle of blood on the floor in front of the prisoner.

Elaine, the matron, leaned over Ashlee. "You'd better get your butt up, Ms. Anderson," she said quietly. "You might be able to fool your lawyer, but I'm not buying this act."

Gerald banged on the window.

Elaine grabbed the phone swinging dangerously close to her head.

"What?" she barked.

"Get my client to the hospital. Can't you see she's badly hurt? If she suffers additional physical harm, I'll—I'll sue the department!"

Elaine glared into the man's eyes. "You need to leave NOW. If you don't leave of your own accord, I'll have a couple of the officers escort you out." She slammed the phone into the receptacle on the wall and knelt down, placing her first and second fingers on Ashlee's wrist. Leaning close to the dark head on the floor, she whispered vehemently, "Get your ass up, you faker. He might buy this, but I don't."

When the body on the floor didn't move, Elaine felt her stomach turn over.

*I can't believe this little bitch is going to get away with this. I'd better get a hold of someone and get her moved out of here, now.*

She detached the two-way radio from her belt and, reaching the front desk, told them to call the paramedics. Leaning down, she placed her hand against Ashlee's damp, cold face. She glanced up into the pale, wide-eyed face of the lawyer. As she rose from the floor, he slipped out the door into the corridor. Elaine waited until the paramedics arrived then slipped out of the room and headed back to her office. *God, the paperwork I'm going to have to fill out on this. I'll be so glad when we take this pain-in-the-butt to prison.*

~ * ~

Gerald wandered into the central lobby in time to hear the desk sergeant call for the paramedics. He approached the desk. The inner door swung open, and two young men wearing firefighter uniforms appeared pushing a gurney.

"Sergeant? I'd like to accompany my client to the hospital," he said.

"Not likely, sir," said the sergeant.

"Why not?"

"She's still a prisoner, counselor. You may go to the hospital and meet her there, but I won't permit you to ride in the ambulance."

"I'm sure I don't need to remind you not to ask questions without my presence," he told the sergeant.

"Yeah, yeah. She won't be asked any questions until you show up. All right, Mr. Ingram?" The sergeant's bored response irritated Gerald, but he ground his teeth and walked toward the parking area in front of the Sheriff's Office.

"I should have known Ms. Anderson was too delicate to handle all the facts quite yet," Gerald muttered as he opened his car. Inside the vehicle, he slammed his hands on the steering wheel. "I shouldn't have told her. Damn it."

He sighed deeply then headed back to the Public Defender's office to write his report.

~ * ~

Riona closed the door to the visitor's area and leaned against the wall. *I have to hand it to the woman; she's a good actress. She has her lawyer believing she's innocent. I need some unbiased background. I wonder if I can get Detective Williams to talk to me about Ashlee Anderson.*

The thought of Corey Williams put a smile on Riona's face. The scoundrel had towed her motorcycle, but she couldn't shake the memory of the sun glinting off the gray hair beginning to grace his temples. His shy smile had melted Riona's resistance the minute she saw him, but she could sense his trepidation. *Maybe I can use a little persuasion to get him to talk to me. Can't hurt to try.*

She walked the corridor to the reception area and faced the smirking desk sergeant.

"Yes? May I help you?"

"My name is Riona Byrne. I'm a reporter with the Billington Bulletin. I'm covering a story about Ms. Ashlee Anderson and would like to get some background from a reliable source. Is Detective Williams available for a minute or two?"

"I'll see."

Riona listened to the sergeant's short monosyllabic answers as she glanced about the lobby.

"If you'll just take a seat over there," the sergeant pointed to the reception area, "Detective Williams will be with you shortly."

Riona moved to a chair and began to evaluate the show she'd just witnessed. *That's the only way I can describe it. I sure can't say I was an active participant.* She picked up a magazine and flipped through the pages. Toward the middle of the magazine, she stopped. He stared out from the page; his flaxen hair peeking out from under the cap of a Russian captain's uniform. The blue gray eyes still mesmerized her. She'd forgotten the dimple in his tanned chin was so deep. She quickly found the caption: *Captain André Martichev of the Russian Army helps children to remember what it's like to be a child.* He stood holding a soccer ball under one arm and the hand of an Afghan child in the other. Riona gently ran a finger over the ruggedly tanned face staring up from the page.

"How I miss you, my love," she whispered.

"Uhm, excuse me." Corey shifted uncomfortably.

Riona started. She'd been so engrossed in the picture she hadn't heard him walk up.

"You wanted to see me?" He noted the cover of the Newsweek magazine as she tossed it onto the table.

"Yes. If you have a moment?" Riona stood and looked into the warmth of the hazel eyes surveying her face.

"Sure. Why don't we go to my office?"

The sergeant jumped up from the desk. "She what? Damn, I'll call the paramedics. Have Patrolman Lee follow the ambulance and stand guard. Can you tackle the reports? Good. Thanks, Elaine."

"Is there a problem?" Corey's back straightened, and Riona watched his jaw muscles tighten.

"No, Detective. That damn… Ms. Anderson has injured herself enough to need stitches. Nothing to worry about, sir. I've got it handled."

"Well, if there's anything I can do…"

"I'll give you a call, sir. Thank you." The sergeant nodded to Corey.

"Anytime. Miss Byrne? After you." Corey opened the door and ushered her through. He led her down the hallway and into an office, shutting the door behind them. The half glass walls offered a view of the entire floor, and Riona noted several heads poke up over partitions. They quickly disappeared when Corey looked out.

"What is it I can do for you?" he asked. His heart fluttered as his mind raced with the possibilities. *Ask anything.*

"I've just witnessed a performance by Ms. Anderson. It was entertaining, to say the least, but I just don't buy it. I'd like some information about her. I read you were the lead detective on the case. Is there anything you can tell me?" She leaned forward placing her notepad on the desktop, pencil poised to write.

Corey shifted his bulk in the chair. "I'm not sure I can offer you much help. I'm bound by the court and District Attorney not to discuss the case before the trial. I can offer some insights to Ms. Anderson apart from the trial. I've lived in Oakdale all my life and so has she, although I don't see how that will help your article."

"The only articles I could find that mention Ashlee Anderson were pretty acidic, and didn't try to hide the distaste the reporter felt for her. As a newsperson, I believe there are two sides to every story. Even Ted Bundy was presented as a likable guy by some of the reporters who questioned him. Now, I'm not saying Ms. Anderson is as ruthless as Ted Bundy, but the stories I've read sure make her sound as vicious. I can't believe a nice guy like Justin Anderson would fall for a girl so cruel." Riona leaned back in the chair. "There has to be another side. I was hoping you might be able to shed some light on the subject or show me where to look."

Corey placed his elbows on the sides of his chair and templed his fingers under his chin. "I'll give you some of what you want on one condition," he said.

Riona's stomach began to flutter. She could see the beginnings of a smile at the corners of the detective's mouth.

"Okay, I'll bite. What's your condition?" She looked into his twinkling hazel eyes.

"I can't say anything here in the office. Let's meet at Sallianne's Diner for coffee in about an hour. Okay?" He grinned.

"Okay, but only because I need this story." Riona rose from the chair.

Corey opened the door and walked behind her to the lobby. He watched her stride out the front doors; her easy gait music to his eyes. *I'm going to enjoy every minute of this.* He moved to the table and picked up the magazine she'd been reading. He had to find out what there was about this old copy of Newsweek that had captured her attention. He remembered a man in a uniform.

*Who is he and why did he have such an effect on her?* There were so many things about this dynamic spitfire Corey wanted to know but, right now, he needed to get back to his office and spruce up. In one hour, he had a date with a tall red-haired angel.

# Eight

Riona pushed her way through the doors of the sheriff's station and into the stifling heat. Her long, even steps brought her quickly to her truck. She felt the rivulets of water trickle between her ample breasts as she swung herself into the cab and started the engine. *A few moments inside the air conditioning and I should be able to calm my thoughts and quit sweating like a workhorse.*

A quick flip of the knob lowered the temperature. Soon, the air circulating inside her cab was cool and refreshing, unlike the swirling maelstrom hotly fogging her mind. She closed her eyes and sucked in deep breaths of cool air.

"I'd stopped thinking of you every day, André. Now this," Riona allowed a tear to streak down her cheek and plop on her shoulder. "I miss you so much. Do you realize, my love, we could be married, and no one would care? Times have changed so much since you left, but I still have a piece of you with me." She reached to her throat and stroked the silver unicorn then turned the engine off and resettled in the seat.

*There's still time before I have to meet the detective. I wonder why he isn't married. Oh, knock it off, Riona.*

Riona ran her fingers over the smooth unicorn hugging the base of her throat as she felt the tension drain from her body. She sighed and gave into the downward tugging of her eyelids. The outside noises faded away, leaving only the even whisper of Riona's breathing in the cab.

~ * ~

*Afghanistan, 1980s*

Four men crouched near the open fire, stretching out their hands toward the warmth.

"If I am to die, I would wish it to be in Moscow where the women aren't covered head to toe, and I can pronounce the names of everything. I didn't join the army to come to Afghanistan. The only thing here is dust—everywhere, dust." Alexei spat on the dirt floor.

"Da, the women you may see, but most of them wouldn't have a thing to do with you." Ilya's white smile contrasted against his dirt-covered face.

"I was drafted even though I flunked the physical. I shouldn't even be here," Serge grumbled as he tossed another piece of wood into the fire pit.

"My Tatiana has just had our first born—a son—and they wouldn't let me spend a weekend with my new child and wife. The way things are going he'll be fighting these blasted Mujahadeen. What I wouldn't give for a hot bath," Vladislav sighed.

The door burst open and a hunched figure stumbled through, grappling to catch the handle and close it before the wind extinguished the fire.

"Close the door, you idiot. Were you born in a stable?" Serge started to rise from his coveted spot around the fire. His woolen floor length coat opened slightly to reveal tan khakis tucked into canvas and leather boots.

"Be careful who you call a stable rat, Serge. Welcome, Captain Martichev." Sergeant Major Uri Petrovich stood at attention. The four men crouching at the fire jumped up and followed his example.

"It's alright, Sergeant. I would suspect the stable rats in this city might be warmer and better fed. At ease, gentlemen, don't let me interrupt. A word, Sergeant?" Captain Andre Martichev took his hat off and brushed the dust from the top.

"Yes, sir." Sergeant Petrovich continued to stand as the captain moved toward him.

"Uri?"

"Yes sir?"

"Can we talk openly here? Is it safe?"

"Da. I trust my life to these men. They know I would slit their throats if they talked." He glanced in the direction of the four men huddled around the fire quietly conversing.

"Have you met the new reporter who showed up in camp last week?" The captain examined the bill of the hat in his hands.

"Yes, why?" The sergeant narrowed his eyes at his commanding officer.

"I don't know, but something doesn't seem quite right. His voice seems high; maybe it's just the Irish accent. I watched him drinking with a couple of tank commanders, and he seemed to hold his own, but something just doesn't fit. Do you know what I mean?"

"Da. I got the same feeling when I met him. We'll keep an eye on him, and I'll report anything unusual to you." The sergeant clicked his heels together and saluted the captain.

The captain returned the salute. "Thank you. I appreciate it. Well, I have to return to my quarters before my lieutenant starts worrying about me like an old woman. I'd like a progress report within the week."

The captain nodded to the men around the fire and, struggling with the door, ventured out into the tempest.

Sergeant Petrovich reclaimed his chair and settled in, crossing his arms over his chest. He would pursue the reporter tomorrow. Tonight, for the first time in three weeks, he'd had enough to eat, and he was warm. He might be able to get a couple hours restful sleep. He was sure going to try.

~ * ~

Riona's body jerked, her eyes flew open and she felt the chill advancing down her spine, one vertebra at a time. Her hand stretched out to turn off the truck but the ignition was already switched to that position. She reached for the air conditioning controls but stopped, her hand poised over the knobs as she reasoned, if the truck was off, the air conditioning was too. The chill crept down her spine again. She grabbed her steno pad and purse and escaped the cab of her vehicle. Watching the heat rise in waves from the pavement, Riona shivered. A step away from the truck and the hot sticky air began to weigh heavy on her. Riona crossed the town square in less than a minute and entered the coolness of Sallianne's Coffee Shop.

"You alright, hon?" the waitress, wearing the nametag Sallianne, asked.

"Yeah, I'm fine. Listen, I'm supposed to meet Corey Williams here. Has he arrived yet?" Riona's gaze swept the coffee shop.

"Yeah, he's in the corner booth." As Sallianne turned to point out the booth, a hand appeared, waving at the back of the shop.

"I see him. Thanks." Riona headed toward the farthest point of the shop. The waitress, menus under one arm, coffee pot in the other, followed her to a booth halfway down the aisle where she stopped and refilled the coffee cups of two older ladies.

*Good. He's chosen someplace discreet.*

Riona felt her ears pop, and a sizzling sound drowned out the country western song coming from the overhead speakers. Little black spots began to appear in front of her eyes and, by the time she'd reached the table, her vision had become blurry as she dropped into the nearest seat. The figure across the table was fuzzy and everything was beginning to blend together.

"Ms. Byrne? Are you all right? You don't look very well." Corey's low voice was a rumble of sound against a sea of color.

Riona opened her mouth to respond but could only sigh and give in to the blackness overcoming her, as she fell across the seat of the booth.

"Sallianne!" Corey shouted. "Call Doc Turley."

Sallianne trotted down the aisle, rounding the end of the counter as she set the coffee pot on the burner, and reached for the phone underneath. A figure sitting on the end stool rose.

"Sallianne, don't bother. I'm right here, however if you'd get me a cool damp cloth and a glass of ice shavings, I'd appreciate it." The young doctor strode to where Corey was pacing in front of the booth. The perplexed expression on the detective's face caused the corners of doctor Turley's mouth to turn up in amusement.

"What's the problem, Corey?" He leaned over the woman stretched across the booth's seat.

"I don't know, Doc," he said. "When she came in for our meeting, she looked really wobbly walking down the aisle. Her face got white, her eyes rolled back, then she just fell over."

"Well, you know a lot of outsiders just can't handle the humid Virginia summers. Maybe she's one of them. She is very fair." The young doctor had been checking Riona's pulse and testing the feel of the skin on her face and arms. *Cold and clammy, just like I thought.*

"I think what we have is a simple case of heat exhaustion. When Sallianne gets here, we'll bring her around and go from there."

The waitress had walked up behind the doctor and, at the mention of her name, handed him the cool cloth and glass of ice chips. She also handed him a plain glass of water.

"Good idea, Sallianne. Glad you thought of it." The young doctor turned and smiled at her.

"Thanks, Doc. Corey, you need anything?" Her eyebrows rose in question.

"Yeah, can you warm up my coffee?"

"Sure thing."

The doctor gently laid the cool cloth on the back of Riona's neck as he picked up an ice chip and rubbed it across her lips. A groan escaped between the dry lips, a pink tongue slipping out and circling the area the doctor had just covered. The deep auburn lashes began to flutter and soon a pair of confused deep brown eyes stared at the underside of the table.

"What the—?" Riona attempted to prop her elbow beneath her.

"I wouldn't try getting up just yet, ma'am." Doctor Turley touched her arm. "You're still a bit flushed and, until we get some liquid down you, I'd prefer you didn't move too fast. Guess our Virginia summer is a little much for you."

"I've survived summer in Kabul. I think I can survive summer here," she muttered.

Corey had stopped pacing and listened to the exchange between the doctor and Riona. *Kabul. Why does that name sound so familiar?*

He watched her ivory skin begin to glow as she sucked on the ice chips. Soon the doctor allowed her to straighten herself to a sitting position. Corey felt his shoulders relax, and he quit clenching his fists. The sparkle returned to the big brown eyes framed in auburn lashes.

"Whew. I must have fallen asleep in the cab of my truck and it got warmer than I expected. I'm not the fainting type." She leaned against the seat back and allowed herself to relax. "Helluva way to start an interview." She smiled weakly. "I'm fine now, Doc. You can finish your coffee."

Doctor Turley checked her pulse again and put the palm of his hand to her forehead.

"You're not as warm as you were ten minutes ago, but I would suggest you keep your activity to a minimum today. I think I'll take your advice and finish my coffee now. However, miss, if you start feeling ill again call my office. Here's my card." The doctor placed his card on the table in front of Riona and returned to his seat at the counter.

"That's the first time I've done that." Riona smiled at Corey, now sitting across from her.

"Are you sure you want to continue with this?" Corey's brow furrowed with concern.

"Of course. I have to turn in my story to the paper by two, and this little incident has cost me precious time. What can you tell me about Ashley Anderson?" Riona picked up her pen and moved her steno pad under her hand.

"I can't tell you a whole lot because this is an ongoing case." Corey turned the cup of coffee in his fingers.

"So this was just an excuse to get me to sit down and have coffee with you. Is that it?" Riona watched the man across from her redden and squirm in his seat.

"Well, uh, I, uh, uh, can tell you a few things about when we were growing up." Corey looked into her twinkling eyes. He shifted his gaze to the quickly cooling brew in his cup. *Damn! She makes me feel like a self-conscious teenager again. Why is her opinion so important to me?*

Riona bit her lips together and tried to keep from laughing at the detective. *He's adorable. I haven't seen a man blush in—I don't know how long. I think I could like him.*

"That would be great. I need some background to help me decide how to write this piece. It's pretty hard when everyone is town has such a definite idea of Ashlee's guilt or innocence. There's not too many who think she's innocent. It makes me wonder why," she said.

"Ashlee started out from a wealthy family but her father made some bad business deals and, before the end of her junior year in high school, she was working after school like the rest of us. She regarded everyone else as *beneath* her and had no problem letting us know. So when she got herself in this compromising position, the riff-raff she's tried so hard to avoid loved every uncomfortable minute. If they thought they could get away with lynching her, a mob would form outside the jail tonight. I'm afraid my friend Justin was taken in by her ice blue eyes and pouty lips. She can be absolutely charming when she wants something." Corey signaled for the waitress.

Sallianne ambled back to the booth. "Ya want some more, hon? How about you, sugar? You ready for something to drink now?"

Riona considered for a moment. "I think I'll have some of that sweet tea with lots of ice."

"One ice tea slush coming up. I'll bring you back a fresh pot of coffee, Corey."

He nodded and leaned against the back of the booth. "You have any questions?"

Riona looked over her notes. She chewed the corner of her bottom lip as she reread what she'd written.

Corey watched her carefully. *I'd love to chew the corner of your lip for you. Whoa. I'd better watch it or I'll give myself away.* He pushed the coffee cup to the edge of the table. Sallianne appeared carrying a coffee pot and glass of tea. She put the tea in front of Riona and filled Corey's cup. Turning, she hustled down the aisle. The booths and counter of the small diner were filling with customers arriving for lunch. The insignificant background noise when Corey and Riona had begun their conversation was rising with each newcomer. Dishes clattered and the ringing of the cook's bell was almost constant. Two other waitresses materialized from the back room, and the diner buzzed with the lunch crowd.

"Actually, I..." Riona started.

"What? I'm sorry but I'm having a hard time hearing you over the din." Corey shrugged his shoulders.

Riona grinned. *He really is adorable.* She cleared her throat and spoke up. "I think that'll help me for now. I can research through the paper and library for any other information I need. Since I was assigned to take over the story after the first reporter left town, I have a lot of notes I can use." She flipped the steno pad closed and sipped her tea.

"Is that how you met Justin and Diane?" Corey asked.

"Yeah, I was assigned to cover the gas leak story. Getting to know those two was a nice benefit. I like them. They're no nonsense people who've seen a lot and still took a chance on love." Riona swirled the tea and ice with the straw.

"Yeah, well, not everybody's as lucky as Justin. Diane is one of a kind. Most women aren't like her." Corey looked out across the square.

"Sounds like you've been badly burned." Riona watched the detective's face.

"You could say that." He didn't give away the boiling in his stomach.

"Want to talk about it?"

He smiled. As he opened his mouth to answer, his beeper sounded. Sighing, he pulled the little black box from his belt and peered at the readout window. "Well, Miss Byrne, duty calls."

He pulled a business card from his pocket and slid it across the table toward her. "Should you need anything else, please don't hesitate to call me." He moved to the edge of the seat, stood, and walked down the aisle.

Moments later, Riona watched his purposeful strides as he crossed the square.

*What a dichotomy. He seems so sure of himself when he's being the detective and so totally unsure of himself around me. Maybe, I make him nervous.* She grinned. "It's been a long time since I had that effect on a man. This could be fun."

She gathered her belongings and went to the register to pay.

Sallianne waved her off. "Corey already got it. You take care now, hon, don't overdo it, and come back to see us soon." Pulling a pencil from behind her ear, Sallianne flipped back the pages of her order pad on her way to another table.

Riona pushed out into the morning, sucking air through her teeth as the waves of heat engulfed her. She strolled to her truck and started the engine and air conditioning. She couldn't afford to lose any more time to something as foolish as heat stroke.

She'd been telling the truth when she'd told Corey she had a two o'clock deadline. She put the truck in gear and headed for Billington and the town library. There was more to this story than Corey was telling her, but she'd have to dig it out herself. She flipped on the police scanner sitting on the seat. The speaker crackled with activity.

"That's different. This thing is usually quiet. Wonder if this has anything to do with the excitement at the police station?" She turned the volume up and listened as the officers communicated back and forth. Finding the first driveway she could, she turned the truck around and started back to Oakdale. She recognized the voice speaking.

~ * ~

"What the hell happened to her after the reporter left?" Corey's anger seethed through his voice.

"I don't know, sir," an unidentified voice squeaked.

"Well, find out and get back to me immediately," Corey barked.

"Yes, sir."

*Her? Who were they referring to?*

Oakdale was a small community and there could only be one *her* being held in the jail—Ashlee Anderson. Riona sped up. The paper would wait for this story.

## Nine

Corey sucked in a breath. He'd only been in the coffee shop for forty-five minutes and it felt like the temperature had risen ten degrees. A rivulet of sweat raced down his back.

*I need to get inside before I melt into a puddle of ooze or die of heat exhaustion. No wonder Riona passed out. Sallianne keeps the air conditioning in the coffee shop on Artic.*

His determined strides quickly brought him to the police department. He pushed through the doors and moved toward the jail section. The square of his shoulders and set of his jaw deterred the desk sergeant from making a comment about his date.

"Get hold of Kurt Lee, right now," Corey tossed the command to the sergeant as he walked past him.

"Yes, sir."

"Have him report to me immediately."

"Yes, sir."

Corey stood until the sergeant buzzed him through the locked door. He glanced inside the matron's office. The desk chair had fallen, or been pushed over, and the cluttered desktop appeared to have accumulated more paperwork since the last time Corey had stopped in to confer with Elaine on the welfare of the jail's only female inmate. The matron stood, shoulders hunched forward at the desk.

Corey, standing in the doorway, growled at Elaine, "How the hell did this happen?"

"I—I don't know, sir. She was conferring with her lawyer and that reporter when I heard him shouting. I went running to the visitor section and found her on the floor bleeding. I called the paramedics right away."

"Well, she'll be in the hospital where they'll want to watch her overnight. I suggest you gather your things and head for home, Sergeant Madison. You get to watch over our guest on the graveyard shift. You might want to get some sleep before then."

Corey turned on his heel and marched to the front desk.

"Have we heard from Kurt Lee?" he asked.

"Yes, sir. He's on line three for you."

Corey picked up the phone on the sergeant's desk.

"Kurt, stay with Ashlee," Corey said. "I'll be there shortly."

Patrolman Lee, following the paramedics unit in his police car, had tailed them to the hospital. After the emergency room doctor determined Ashlee's injury was not life threatening, she was stitched up and placed in a secured wing.

Corey drove over from the station. He leaned against the wall, waiting for the nurse to finish taking her blood pressure and giving Ashlee pain medication. When she'd finished her ministrations, the nurse left the room to the prisoner and the detective.

Corey pulled a chair up to the side of the bed. "What happened? Couldn't you sweet-talk your attorney into getting what you wanted?"

Ashlee's mouth flattened into a thin line and her eyes burned with contempt. After a few seconds of complete silence, she turned toward the wall.

"You can turn away from me but the truth doesn't disappear quite so easily. I'll be back tomorrow when you feel better, and we'll have a friendly discussion on how you accomplished this little feat." He pushed the chair against the wall and left.

~ * ~

Patrolman Kurt Lee watched the detective lumber down the hospital corridor and push his way through the doors at the end. He waited five minutes and slipped into Ashlee's room.

"Where the hell have you been?" Ashlee spat out the whispered question.

"I had to wait until I was sure Detective Williams had left the floor." Kurt walked over to the window and, lifting the slats in the mini-blind, watched the detective's hulking red truck drive out of the hospital parking lot.

"He's gone for now," he said.

"Yeah, but he'll be back tomorrow bright and early. You can count on it." Ashlee straightened herself in the bed.

"I thought they gave you something to sleep." Kurt watched her rearrange the sheets around herself.

Ashlee held out her hand to him. The center held a red capsule. "They did. I just didn't swallow. I figure it will come in handy later. Now… have you got everything we need to get the hell out of here?"

"Shhhhhhh. Ashlee, don't talk so loud." Kurt scanned the room.

"Kurt," Ashlee shook her head. "I made sure there weren't any cameras when we got in here. I sure wouldn't be flashing this little pill around if I thought they were going to force it down my throat because they'd been watching me on some monitor at the nurse's station. Man, you're jumpy. Have you got everything?" She was gingerly fingering the bandage on her forehead.

"Yes, I've got a passport and two open-ended airline tickets. When are you planning on executing this getaway?" Kurt sat on the end of the bed.

"I thought I might get a few hours of sleep. I heard the nurse say Sergeant Madison drew duty at midnight, so a distraction shortly before one, and my little red knockout pill shoved down the sergeant's throat should give us five to six hours head start on anyone who might feel the need to follow. That sound alright to you?" The ice blue eyes surveyed Kurt.

"Sounds like it'll work. I'll get back to my *official* duties and check in with you before she shows up." Opening the door, he peered up and down the hall then slipped back to his post. A quick glance at his watch told him it was nine thirty. He had two and a half hours before Sergeant Madison took over his watch. Another look down the hallway and Kurt spotted a nurse moving in his direction. Folding his fingers into a fist, he thumped the wall twice.

The nurse, pulling the chart from the holder by the door, looked up at the officer standing on the other side, her raised eyes questioning. He smiled. "Department's got a lot to lose if this one gets away."

"I doubt she's going very far, officer, those sleeping pills we give the patients are strong to be sure they get the rest they need. She'd have to be psychotic to throw off the effects. I'm going to check her vitals then be on my way. Excuse me."

Kurt opened the door for the nurse and glanced at the patient in the bed. Ashlee looked as though she had been sleeping for an hour. If he hadn't been talking to her five minutes earlier, he wouldn't have known she wasn't under the influence of the pill.

The nurse entered and gently shook Ashlee. "Miss? I need to get your blood pressure and temperature. I won't be long."

Ashlee mumbled something inaudible and rolled flat on her back. The nurse slipped a jacketed thermometer under her tongue and pumped the blood pressure cuff wrapped around Ashlee's arm. Noting the temperature and blood pressure on the chart, the nurse carefully covered the patient and exited the room to the hallway.

"Well, is she going to live?" Kurt asked.

"Yes, officer, she seems to be doing fine. All her vitals are normal." The nurse scribbled something on the chart and slipped it into the holder.

"You're going to check her hourly?"

"No. Since Ms. Anderson seems to be doing so well, I've noted her vitals won't need to be taken again until around midnight. However, that'll be a different nurse because my shift ends at eleven. Since I won't see you again, have a nice evening, officer."

"You, too, ma'am." Kurt watched the nurse repeat the same routine at each room down the corridor. When she passed by him on her way out, he checked the time. It had taken the nurse an hour to complete her rounds. She spent about five minutes in each room and a minute writing on the chart outside the room. He began calculating.

~ * ~

Elaine Madison reached out blindly, trying to pinpoint the annoying buzz jangling her taut nerves. Unsuccessful, she pushed herself into a sitting position and located the offending source. Smacking the top of the radio alarm clock, a silence flooded the cool, darkened bedroom. Elaine groaned at the glowing red numbers on the face of the clock.

"Damn. It's eleven thirty, and I have the distinction of standing guard over the Hypochondria Queen. I'll be glad when this trial is over, and the State takes her off our hands. For once, I think Ms. Ashlee Anderson is going to get exactly what she deserves." Elaine grinned as she snapped on the lamp, squinting and grimacing in the sudden light. Muttering continuously, she dressed then drove to the hospital.

*With any luck, this will be the last time I have to spend the night with Ashlee Anderson.*

~ * ~

Corey shuffled the paperwork on his desk.

"I know that transcript is here—somewhere," he mumbled as he moved papers from one side of the desk to the other. "Aha! Here it is."

The tab on the manila folder read: *Jury Trial, Thomas Manning, Sr. June 17.*

"It's in this transcript somewhere. Something here has been driving me crazy and hanging this feeling of foreboding over my head." Corey flipped through a dozen pages and stopped. He turned back one page and began to read:

*Q: "Were you expecting anyone to meet you at the cabin?"*

*A: "Yes. Ashlee was supposed to pick up dinner and bring it back to the cabin."*

*Q: "Why didn't you just eat at the restaurant?"*

*A: "After I'd introduced her to the man I thought was a hit man and we'd concluded our business, she and I went into the restaurant for dinner. But Ashlee was acting very... uhm, well, amorous. She hadn't been this affectionate in a long time. When she suggested we take dinner back to the cabin and continue our discussion, I didn't argue. I said I wanted to do a little housekeeping before she came over, and she agreed to wait until the food was ready. I drove to the cabin, cleaned the place up, and was waiting for her to show up, when the police arrived."*

Corey sat for a moment and replayed the evening in his mind. This was close to what he was looking for, but wasn't exactly the right question and answer session. He flipped through the transcript and stopped a few pages later. After a brief reading, the hair on the back of his neck stood up. This section held his answer. He reread it:

*Q: "Officer Lee, you were on duty at the reception desk in the station on the night in question, weren't you?"*

*A: "Yes, sir, I was."*

*Q: "Did you have occasion to call Ms. Anderson?"*

*A: "No, sir."*

*Q: "Let me advise you, Officer, you were seen on a cell phone immediately after the call was made to arrest Mr. Manning at the cabin. You weren't on the phone to Ms. Anderson?"*

*A: "No, sir, I was calling my wife to let her know I had just made dinner reservations for our anniversary the following Saturday night."*

Corey looked up from the transcript. He remembered looking at Kurt's wife and noting the expression of surprise pass over her face. She'd quickly assumed a non-committal look. At the time he'd wondered what had triggered her response but didn't dwell on it. Now it began to make sense.

"Damn it!" Corey glanced at the small clock on his desk. Twelve thirty. He needed to call the hospital. He picked up the phone book then dialed the general number.

Once connected to the secure unit, he talked with the nurse on duty.

"This is Detective Corey Williams from the Oakdale Police. I'm verifying the condition of a prisoner that was brought in today. A Ms. Ashlee Anderson? Have there been any changes with her status?"

"No, Detective. Rounds were last done about, oh, nine thirty, and the patient was resting. Her vital signs were normal. The officer is still present outside the room and I don't really think there'll be a problem. The sleeping pills have a tendency to put the patient to sleep for at least twelve hours. We have your number here and if anything occurs out of the ordinary, I'll contact you. Goodnight."

*Well, everything seems all right. Why do I have this imminent feeling of dread?*

He reasoned, *I've been working since seven o'clock this morning, and I'm just tired.* Straightening his desk, he turned off his desk lamp and headed out the door toward home.

*A good night's sleep will help everything. I'll turn the air conditioning up and drift away. Maybe tomorrow I can contact Riona and see how she's feeling. I'd sure like a chance to have coffee without a crisis.*

Once home, he cranked up the air until his room was cool enough to sleep comfortably, then dropped into bed.

~ * ~

Four a.m. In the predawn darkness, Corey Williams bolted upright from a restless sleep. *I have it! I know the identity of the department's inside leak.*

# Ten

Riona turned on her side and flung her arm in the direction of the nightstand and the buzzing alarm. She rested her hand on the alarm and realized there were no vibrations emanating from the small box. Her body relaxed, and she began to drift back to sleep when the obnoxious sound aroused her again. *What the hell is going on?*

Riona squinted at the luminescent numbers displayed on the clock. *Four fifteen. I must be dreaming.* Allowing her body to settle on the bed, she jumped when the incessant buzzing began again. She struggled through the fog of sleep and pulled herself to a sitting position. *Phone. It's the damn phone.*

She snatched the cell off the nightstand. "This had better be damned good to get my ass up at four fifteen in the morning. Hello? HELLO?"

The phone clicked silent. "Damn it!"

Hurling the small instrument across the room, it struck the wall and thudded to the floor. Awake and irritated, Riona got up and padded into the kitchen. *I've been out of the field too long. I've gotten soft and stopped listening to my gut. Something about this whole situation stinks. I've let myself be sidetracked by a man again. The last time it happened was in Afghanistan with André.*

Water ran into the coffee carafe as Riona stared blindly out the window over the sink, while memories flooded her mind, and a tear escaped down her cheek.

~ * ~

The Russian captain turned the collar of his overcoat up and scrunched his neck into the wool warmth. He hurried along the pathway to his commandeered office and living quarters. His mind busily working on the next day's line of defenses, he didn't see the tall weaving figure until a moment before the collision.

The figure barreled into the captain, stumbled, and fell backwards onto the dusty pathway. Captain Martichev tottered but kept his balance. He leaned over and extended a hand to the figure in the dirt.

"Why don't ya watch where the bloody hell yer goin'?" The figure looked up at the captain and slapped away the offered hand. "Great, a Ruskie."

It took the captain a moment to recognize the heavily accented English.

"My apologies. Let me offer a hand and help you to find your dwelling. It's very dangerous for a civilian to be out this late at night without a military escort. Where may I drop you?"

The figure on the ground struggled, finally rising from the dirt. "I wuz doin' jus' fine til you knocked me down. I can fin' my own room." The intoxicated loner then fell face-forward into the dust.

Captain Martichev knelt down, and turning the figure on its back, searched the overcoat pockets. Retrieving a flashlight, he flicked the beam on, obscuring the reflection with his body.

The press identification put a name to the limp body on the ground, Ron Byrne, and he recognized the key from the hotel where the world press stayed in Kabul. *Well, Ron Byrne, if you're stupid enough to get drunk in a Muslim country and wander the streets alone at night, maybe I should let you get your throat slit for the few dollars in your wallet. I would, but my grandmother would haunt me until the day I die.*

Sliding his arm under the drunken reporter, the captain lifted the limp body. Clinging to the shadows of the buildings, he maneuvered the narrow dirt pathways until he reached the town plaza. Glancing warily at the space, he sucked in a large breath and walked as calmly as he could across the openness. A clerk looked up from the desk as the captain entered. His face registered nothing but the unending boredom suffered by all hotel clerks. He lowered his head to continue reading. The captain trudged up two flights of stairs to the reporter's room. He wrestled the key into the lock only to find the door pushed open. A short walk to the bed and with one shrug of his shoulder, he set the reporter on his back on the bed. The captain had turned to leave when he heard the groan.

"Mmmmbbbddd," Ron mumbled.

"Excuse me?" The captain leaned closer to hear.

He was grabbed and pulled on top of the reporter, who locked him in an embrace, kissing him passionately. The captain found himself responding. *Whoa! This is a man. What am I doing?* Captain Martichev grappled with the reporter and freed himself. He bolted to the door, shutting it tightly behind him. He was shaken at his response to the reporter. *I have been here too long. I need to ask for a transfer back to Mother Russia, where there are lots of women. What could I have been thinking?*

~ * ~

Riona smiled at the incident. How could he have known she'd protected her ability to report in a Muslim country by using the nickname the boys in the newsroom had given her—Ron.

Everything Riona had learned in Afghanistan, she'd put aside when she'd moved to Billington. However, something about Ashlee made her insides twist every time Riona thought about her. *There has to be some insider feeding her information. Ashlee's smart but not that smart. I'll get to the bottom of this. I can sense a big story here, and I aim to be the first to get it.*

After pouring water into the holder, and pushing the start button on the coffee machine, Riona padded back into the bedroom.

"I'm up. I might as well take a shower and get dressed. Damn it, I could use a cigarette. What a hell of a time to quit," she mused aloud. Moving toward the bathroom, she jumped at the sound of the phone.

"Where did I throw that stupid thing?" She hunted frantically along the floor of the bedroom. Finding it under the dresser, she flipped open the phone.

"What?"

## Eleven

"Riona? It's Corey."

"Do you realize it's four damn thirty in the morning? You'd better give me a good reason not to hang up."

"How about an exclusive scoop on the story of the year?"

"What story? This had better be worth me staying up."

"I'll guarantee it. I need to clean up first. I also do better with food in my belly. Meet me at Sallianne's around six? We can try having coffee again."

"Listen, bud, you're not making any points with that comment, however, I think better with food in my stomach, too.

I'll see you there."

~ * ~

Officer Elaine Madison emerged from the hospital elevator glowering. She scanned the length of the empty corridor. *I thought Kurt Lee was standing guard over Ashlee. Where the hell is he?*

She started toward the nurse's station, her highly glossed shoes echoing off the walls with each footstep. As she neared the door with the chair placed outside, Kurt Lee stepped from the room.

"Gosh, is it midnight already? Great! I can still get a beer with the guys over at The Bar." Kurt flashed Elaine a smile.

"What the hell were you doing?" She glared at the dimpled tan face.

The door to the room opened and a nurse stood in the doorway until the two police officers parted.

"Goodnight, Kurt." The petite nurse's coy smile made Elaine grit her teeth.

"Goodnight, Wanda. See you tomorrow." Kurt winked.

"What was that all about? Kurt, you're supposed to be watching Ashlee, not putting notches in your belt. You're married, right?" Elaine smirked at the handsome patrolman.

"Married, not dead. Besides, how hard is it to watch a sleeping body? The pills they've given her are guaranteed to knock her out for at least twelve hours. It gets boring just sitting here."

"Life is hard. Your job is to *just sit here* and make sure the prisoner doesn't escape. Ashlee Anderson is quite capable of finding a way to get out of the justice due her. That's why Detective Williams put a guard on her. Are you getting the picture now?" Elaine crossed to the door.

"Man, you've really got it in for Ashlee. What did she ever do to you?" Kurt followed Elaine into the room he had just exited.

"Not that it's any of your business, but if it hadn't been for Ashlee, I would've been Elaine Anderson. She never deserved Justin, but he was stupid enough to fall for those long legs and big blue eyes. I could have told him something like this would happen." Elaine's smug smile was visible in the dimly lit room.

The two officers ventured toward the bed where Ashlee was sleeping.

"What are you doing?" Kurt asked.

"I'm making sure she's still there."

"They gave her a sleeping pill not more than fifteen minutes ago. I stood here and watched her take it myself. She's so far out of it she wouldn't know her own mother. Jeez, Elaine, you're being too paranoid." Kurt shook his head.

She ventured to the edge of the bed and leaned over toward the sleeping figure. She straightened up slightly and a puzzled expression crossed her face. "Something's not quite right here." Elaine turned her head in time to catch a flash of metal.

Kurt whistled softly, and the petite nurse stepped back to watch the figure slump to the ground. Kurt grabbed the matron under her arms as the nurse grabbed the legs. With one smooth effort, they rolled her onto the hospital bed. Elaine groaned softly.

"How are we gonna get her to take those pills?" Kurt asked.

"Shut up and give me a hand. You know how to strip a woman, don't you?" Ashlee began to undress the matron.

Kurt took off her shoes and socks and unbuckled her belt. "We don't have to strip her naked, do we?" He grimaced at the thought.

"Look, how much lead time do you want? Personally, I'd prefer a week or two but since that's not possible, I'm giving myself all the time I can. Get her clothes off, get her in a hospital gown, and I'll get these pills down her throat. That should give us at least four to six hours head start. By the time anyone figures it out, we should be in Mexico. Now move it!" Ashlee, dressed in a nurse's uniform, grabbed the clothes and threw them at Kurt. "Here. Put these somewhere. If the figure in the bed looks like me, no one will suspect it's not me."

Kurt hung the clothes over the back of the visitor's chair near the door. He turned to see Ashlee prying open Elaine's mouth. She pushed a pill to the back of the matron's throat and drizzled water down her open mouth. The matron instinctively swallowed. Ashlee performed the same action again with a second pill. Ashlee stepped back and looked at the prone officer.

"You were right, you cow. I was faking it, and you'll never be able to prove it. By the time you come around, I'll be in Mazatlán lying on the beach. Oh, yeah, you would *never* have been Mrs. Anderson."

Ashlee secured Elaine's arms and legs under the sheet and tucked the bottom in, effectively strapping the matron into the bed. "That should keep you for a while," she muttered as she stepped back to admire her handiwork. One last pat on the bed and Ashlee steered Kurt toward the door. She reached but stopped short of grabbing the handle.

"What's the matter now?" Kurt asked.

Eyeing the uniform on the chair, Ashlee answered, "Grab her uniform—all of it."

"Why?"

"Well, getting out of the hospital dressed as a nurse will be no problem, but getting out of the country dressed like a nurse might raise some questions. Nobody will question two police officers flying out of the country, will they?"

"No, I guess not." Kurt picked up the clothes and balled them under his arm.

"You idiot, don't ball them up. Fold them so they don't wrinkle as much. Do I have to do everything myself?"

The pair exited the room and moved down the corridor to the elevator. They made a quick departure out of the air-conditioned building into the sweltering parking lot. Kurt started his truck and began to drive out of the lot with his head lights turned off.

"What are you doing?" Ashlee asked.

"Leaving," he said.

"Without headlights? Have you lost your mind? We're trying not to attract attention. Turn your lights on." Ashlee gritted her teeth. She looked out the window at the dark landscape slipping past. *For the last time, I hope.*

~ * ~

Riona skimmed her fingers through her damp hair. *Hell, it's too hot to use the blow dryer. I'll just let it air dry.*

She'd chosen to wear her emerald summer leathers. A sleeveless cotton shirt under the light vest would keep her cool when the temperature soared to over one hundred later in the day. One small tape recorder loaded with a fresh tape would eliminate the need for a pad and pencil, and might encourage the detective to talk more freely. She slid the slim machine into her inside vest pocket.

She started out the back door and stopped. Her stomach rolled and grumbled. *Yeah, yeah, I'll feed you. God, I could use a cigarette right now.* She stood on the back porch feeling the urge to go, but something held her back. Goose bumps rose on her arms as a rivulet of cold air crept up her spine.

*Something isn't right. I can't put my finger on it but...*

Riona went back inside and double-checked the house. As she stepped onto the porch, the feeling of dread dissipated. *Seems like a really stupid thing to do, but it makes me feel better. Oh, well.*

Tramping to the garage, puffs of soft dirt covered her black riding boots. A quick touch of the button on the opener and the garage opened to reveal the gleaming emerald Harley Davidson. Riona stopped to admire the lines of the sleek machine. *Stops my heart every time I see it. Thank goodness it's mine!*

She climbed on the motorcycle and sped down the driveway. Five o'clock in the morning, the air was still cool enough for Riona to be glad she had worn leathers. Her eyes watered behind the mirrored sunglasses, and she wore a lightly tinted lip-gloss to keep her lips from chapping. Arriving at the diner, she parked the motorcycle and rubbed her numbed ears.

A blast of cool air enveloped her upon opening the diner door. Sizzling bacon sounds greeted her, as sugary syrup and burnt toast smells started to make her mouth water. *Guess I'm hungrier than I thought.* She walked to the booth in the back of the diner. Her coffee, and Corey, arrived simultaneously.

"Coffee black, Carolyn," Corey said to the young waitress.

"You bet, Detective Williams."

Riona watched the detective angle himself into the booth. He turned his hazel eyes her direction. *His eyes look almost green this morning.*

"Your call had the ominous sound of a B movie. What's going on, Detective?"

"Please, call me Corey."

The waitress brought coffee to the table and filled their cups, returning to the kitchen with their breakfast order.

She took a long sip of the black acrid tasting liquid the diner called coffee. Riona knit her brows together. Keeping the relationship with this cop on a business level would be difficult if they used first names, however, she might get a great lead if she let him think she was a little innocent… well, sort of innocent. After all, he had those incredibly beautiful hazel eyes that seemed to change color with the light of day. Where was the harm?

"Only if you call me Riona, Det… Corey." She smiled.

"Good. I'll give you the exclusive on what I think is going to be a big story, but you can't write anything about our discussions until after the trial," he said as he poured three heaping teaspoons of sugar into his cup.

"I'd normally bounce my ideas off my best friend, but he left yesterday for his honeymoon and I don't really want his new wife to hunt me down. She's quite formidable."

"What you're asking is impossible. I have to turn in something every day or I'll lose my job. This is a big waste of my time." Riona started to slide out of the booth.

"No. Please don't go. What I have right now is only a hunch, so there's no physical proof. I can't risk tainting a jury with my hunches. Let me just say four words... *the Ashlee Anderson trial.*" Corey slumped against the back of the booth.

Riona felt a cold draft blow across the back of her neck and the skin on her arms prickled with goose bumps. She slid back inside of the booth.

"Okay, you've got my attention. Something about that woman irritates me to no end. I don't buy the, *everybody-hates-me* routine. So what's happening?" Riona slid her hand into her inside pocket and used her fingernail to flick on the small recorder resting there. She also pulled out a stick of gum and placed it on the table next to her napkin.

Corey leaned toward her. "No tape recorders. This has to be strictly off the record. The minute the trial is over you can print the whole story, but I can't allow anything to get out before the trial. It'll only be for two weeks. Please?"

She moved her hand to her pocket and turned off the recorder.

"I don't know what you know, but if this isn't the biggest story in the state, I'll crucify you and your department." Riona pulled the small machine from her pocket and set it on the table.

"Thanks. I realize I'm asking a lot of you, but I guarantee it will be worth the effort."

Riona stared into the earnest face of the detective. *Cops aren't known for their talents to disclose all the facts. Why do you want so much for me to believe you?*

"I've got everything to lose and nothing to gain. Why don't you confide in your wife?"

"I'm divorced."

"Oh, sorry."

The waitress brought breakfast to the table and conversation halted as they downed eggs, bacon and hot cakes. Coffee cups refilled, the two continued their verbal dance. Corey started.

"How'd you meet Justin and Diane again?" he asked.

"I told this to you yesterday. Weren't you listening?" she said

"Well, uh, kinda. Would you tell me again?" Corey's face was flushing.

"All right, but this is the last time I repeat myself. I was dispatched the first night sabotaged gas lines were discovered at his house. After that, persistence was the key. I called until he agreed to let me interview him. He was such an honest, kind man that I shelved the interview I'd originally planned to print and started focusing my articles from his point of view. After he and Diane got together, we became friends and, as they say, the rest is history," she said.

"Yeah, Justin's a pretty terrific guy, and I'm glad he finally found the right woman. We've known each other since high school. I've also known Ashlee since Justin met her in college. I've felt there's been something I can't put my finger on that makes me uncomfortable around her. You said earlier you didn't buy her *everybody-hates-me* act. You're right—it's an act.

"She has lied, cheated and connived for everything she has, and there's no way she'd allow a man, any man, to get anything over on her. The only thing important in Ashlee's life is Ashlee. That's why my gut is telling me there is something very wrong about this bull she tried to pass off when you were at the jail. Ashlee isn't that fragile."

"So what is it that has you concerned? You know she isn't the delicate butterfly she's pretending to be, but maybe she's worked herself into a state to get out of the jail cell. Some people are claustrophobic."

Riona interlaced her fingers around the empty coffee cup. The young waitress stopped to fill it with fresh hot coffee on her way toward the kitchen. Riona nodded her thanks.

Corey sat back in the booth and crossed his arms. His mouth scrunched to one side. Riona could tell he was chewing the inside of his lip. *He looks like he's trying to decide something important.*

"How'd you feel about taking a trip to the hospital?" he asked.

"I didn't think the food was that bad," Riona smiled.

"I need to check on Ashlee, and I'd like you to go with me. You game?" he said.

"Let's get going." She grabbed the check from the table. "Gotta justify my expense account somehow."

They stood outside in the increasing heat.

"Why don't we lock your bike in the detention yard until we get back?"

"I don't know. I really hate to leave my bike anywhere…" Riona hesitated.

"Well," Corey nodded to the heat waves rising from the sidewalk, "my truck is air-conditioned, and the detention yard is locked and under constant surveillance, but the choice is yours."

"I'll follow you," she said.

Once the emerald Harley had been locked up, the reporter and detective rode to the hospital in silence. As they exited the elevator, Riona sensed Corey tensing. His step quickened until he reached the room with the chair outside the door. Shoving the door open, he ignored the protestations of the nurse who followed him into the room.

"Excuse me. What are you doing in here? This is a secure room." She stood with her feet planted at the foot of the hospital bed.

Corey reached into his pocket and pulled out his identification.

The nurse fingered the badge, handing it to Corey, and moved away toward the door. "Please let me know when you leave."

He opened the door to the small bathroom and peered inside. A frown covered the detective's face.

"What's the problem, Det… Corey?"

"Did you happen to see one of my officers when we came up?" he asked.

"Now that you mention it, no."

A cold draft traveled down Riona's back.

Corey uttered a swear word and moved to the hospital bed. He gently pulled back the sheet on the bed to find himself looking into the gently snoring face of Elaine Madison.

"Damn it. Where the hell is Ashlee Anderson?"

## Twelve

"What!" Riona sprinted to the bed. On the white hospital sheets, puffing little wisps of air through pursed lips; lay the jail matron, Elaine Madison. Riona would never have identified this contented sleeper as the matron of the jail who, the last time she had seen her, appeared crazed and demented enough to kill Ashlee Anderson with her bare hands.

Corey pressed the nurse's button and paced the floor. He glanced at his watch. "Damn it. They have at least six hours head start on us."

Five minutes passed before the nurse appeared at the door. "Yes?"

"I'm Detective Williams." Corey produced his badge. "I'd like some information on the patient admitted to this room. When was the last time she was checked?"

The nurse grabbed the chart from the wall holder. "Her vitals were last taken at four this morning with nothing outside the normal range. I don't see why that should be cause for the police to show up." The nurse checked the chart again and shook her head.

"There's supposed to be a police officer outside this door at all times. The person you have lying in this bed is not the same patient that was admitted."

"You mean this isn't Miss Anderson?"

"No, ma'am. This is Elaine Madison, the police officer assigned to stand guard over the prisoner. Can you or someone on the floor tell me the last time an officer was seen outside this door?" Corey stood arms crossed.

"I'll find someone who was here when the shift changed. I'll be right back."

Corey began to pace in front of the hospital bed. "I can't believe Ashlee just walked out of here. I won't let her get away with trying to murder Justin. What is taking them so long?"

"Corey? You need to slow down and get a little perspective on this. First, let's wait to find out how long she's been gone. Second, who says we can't go after her? Boundaries and areas of responsibility may hinder you, but I have the luxury of going anywhere I want, and this will make a great story. I can get a week's worth of coverage out of this. It'll be the most exciting thing I've covered since I moved here and took a job at the Bulletin." Riona's brown eyes glittered.

"Hold on." Corey gently grasped her arms. "You can't publish anything about this."

"What?" Riona shook his hands free of her arms and stared at him. "Why not?"

"Technically, Ashlee is still in police custody until the trial. I need you to keep this quiet until we find her. I'll contact the lawyers and let them work it out with the judge, but I need to find her. I made a promise to see her go to jail, and I intend to keep my promise. Please, give me a week. After that, you can print anything you want."

Corey looked miserable. Riona rocked back and forth on her feet for a moment, watching him sweat under her gaze. "All right—one week, no more. But tell me, how are you going to keep the hospital staff quiet? Threats? Somebody's going to talk," she said.

"We'll see." Corey stood with his mouth scrunched to one side.

The nurse strode into the room clutching a clipboard. She flipped the pages and ran a finger down to the middle of the page. "Here it is. Sorry, Detective, but everyone from the earlier shift has gone home. There's a note on the night log that, at around twelve thirty, the male officer standing duty walked out with a nurse." The nurse looked up at Corey. "I talked with the on-duty nurse when I came to work this morning and she warned me to stay away from him because he had asked her for a date and walked out with somebody else."

Corey looked at Riona. "Have I got your promise of silence?"

She nodded.

"Thanks miss. You might want to tell your friend that the officer in question is married."

The nurse frowned and, clutching the clipboard under her arm, left the room muttering, "Men are nothing but dogs."

Corey moved to the closet, glanced inside, and stepped out. "Damn it."

Riona raised her eyebrows. "What?"

"The uniform Elaine was wearing is gone. I can only assume Ashlee took it. She'll be able to go anywhere without being challenged. Damn it." Corey slammed his clenched fist into his open hand.

"Well, I guess we'd better start looking for her. Where to now?"

"The station."

Corey and Riona stepped out of the room. He went to the nurse's station and left instructions for the nurses to contact someone at the police station when Elaine awoke. Arrangements would be made to bring clothing for her and find her a ride home.

Corey slid his hand under Riona's arm and escorted her out of the building. His heart pounded with excitement. He loved the cat-and-mouse of the chase, and Ashlee was arrogant enough to think she could outwit him. The corners of his mouth turned up.

"What are you grinning about?" Riona asked.

"The hunt… I love to hunt." Corey smiled.

## Thirteen

Kurt pulled into the parking space and eyed his sleeping passenger. *I sure hope this is worth giving up everything.*

Ashlee stirred and turned to find his questioning eyes searching her face. She leaned toward him and grasped his neck with her hand. Sliding suggestively in his direction, she snuggled up to him, and with a glint in her eyes, she pulled off the nurse's cap and began to unbutton the blouse.

"Not here," Kurt protested.

"Why not?" She slipped the blouse over her shoulders baring her full breasts to his view.

"We… we might get caught." Kurt couldn't take his eyes off the white full mounds being thrust toward him. Ashlee placed his hand on her breast and pushed into him. Kurt moaned.

"Yeah, isn't that a rush?" She slipped her hand down the front of his uniform slacks to caress the ever-growing bulge in his crotch.

"Oh, God…" Kurt allowed himself to be pulled into the physical vortex his body was creating. The couple slipped below the view of the windows.

Twenty minutes later, Ashlee pushed up and lit a cigarette. "Still having doubts?"

Kurt took the cigarette from her hand and pulled smoke deep into his lungs. "Nope."

"Good." She squinted at the building lights twinkling in the distance. "Why did you park so far from the terminal?" she asked.

"I was buying us some time," Kurt said.

"How does parking in the back of the long-term parking lot, out in Timbuktu, buy us time? As far as I can see, it just means we have to walk a couple more miles… unless there's a shuttle." Ashlee brightened at the thought.

"There's a shuttle, alright, but we're not going to make use of it," he answered her.

"And why not?" Even in the semi-darkness of dawn, Kurt could feel Ashlee's frown.

"We need to be as careful as we can about being seen. I came in through the back gate of the airport, which was opened by someone who owed me a favor, and parked back here in Timbuktu, because this is the last place the cops look when they search for missing vehicles. We don't have a stamped parking ticket to place us here at any specific time."

Looking up through her long black lashes, a smile turning the corners of her mouth upward, Ashlee cooed, "I didn't think you could surprise me, Kurt. I was wrong. You do have a brain to go with that beautiful brawn." She reached a manicured finger to his arm and traced a line from his shoulder over his well-formed bicep and down to his hand, where he caught her wrist in his hand.

"Not now, Ashlee. We need to get moving if we're going to put some distance between us and whoever comes to find us."

"Spoil sport." Ashlee looked down at her white uniform. "This worked to get me out of the hospital, but I don't think it will help much getting us past the security checks. Did you remember to bring Elaine's uniform?"

Kurt's brow furrowed. "Of course." He reached behind the seat of his truck and pulled out a bag, which he threw in her direction.

"Turn around while I change."

"What?"

"I *said* turn around while I change." She crossed her arms and stuck out her lower lip.

"Good lord. We just had sex together and you want me to turn around?" Kurt shook his head.

"Do it now, or I won't move a muscle until you do." Ashlee lifted and dropped her crossed arms against her ample chest to emphasize her point.

Sighing, Kurt opened the door of the truck and, grabbing his cigarettes from the dashboard, exited. He turned his back to the cab and lit a smoke while Ashlee changed into the jail matron's uniform. Although the matron was a size larger than Ashlee, a cinched belt kept the pants from falling and Ashlee's larger bosom filled the shirt. She tapped on the window, and he reentered the truck.

"How do I look?" she said.

Kurt reached toward her chest and she shrank from his hand.

"Don't flatter yourself. We don't have time for that. Now sit still." His hand continued to the badge on her pocket flap and turned it in the right direction. He reached past her and pulled a briefcase from under the seat. He snapped open the lid and retrieved a blonde wig and identification badge from inside the case.

"Well, now, aren't you the picture of planning?" she smirked.

"I needed to think of all the possibilities and make sure we gave ourselves the best chance we could to pull this off. Here, put on the wig. I got it on the off chance someone might know her and know she's blonde." He handed the hairpiece to Ashlee.

She pulled the wig over her hair, using the rearview mirror to tuck all the dark ends underneath the cap. A little fussing with the synthetic hair fibers and the transformation was complete.

"How's this?" She moved the mirror back and looked at Kurt.

"You look pretty good as a blonde. Those blue eyes of yours make the hair color work really well." He grinned salaciously. "Wow, I started with a brunette and now I have a blonde. I think I like this."

"As you said earlier, don't get any wild ideas. We don't have time," Ashlee said. "I don't think Corey Williams is buying my sick act. He's never trusted me. I have a sneaking suspicion he'll stop by the hospital on his way to work and discover our little plan."

She looked through the pickup window toward the pinking horizon. "It's getting pretty light. We'd better get going. How do you plan to get us through the airport with these weapons?"

Kurt patted the briefcase. "You'll have to trust me on this, Ashlee," he smirked. "I'll get us through the airport, past the security checks, and on the plane with an escort. Once we're in Mexico you can take over. Until then, I'm holding the key to our freedom. Understood? Now out." Kurt pushed Ashlee toward the door. She stepped down to the parking lot. As the sun began to rise on the horizon, so did the temperature.

Ashlee watched Kurt as he lovingly ran his hand over the back of the seat and across the steering wheel. *If I didn't need you, you weasel, I'd choke the life out of you. I'd almost begun to respect you... almost.*

"Come on," Ashlee hissed. "It's just a damn truck."

"It's been more dependable than any woman I've known." He shut and locked the vehicle. Kurt strode angrily toward the terminal while Ashlee trotted to keep pace with him.

"Would you slow down? Kurt? What is the matter with you?"

She bumped into his back when he stopped and glared down at her. "What is the matter with me? Do you really want to know?"

She crossed her arms and jutted out her chin. "Yeah, I really want to know."

"At this moment, I'm not sure I want to go to Mexico—not with you or anyone else."

"What!"

"I've stolen and falsified paperwork, made the flight reservations and, in general, taken all the chances. All you've been doing is criticizing and complaining. I've got a wife at home who does that same thing day in and day out. I don't need this." He started to push past the small defiant figure.

Ashlee reached out and grabbed Kurt's arm as he started to move away from her.

"Wasn't I worth it an hour ago?"

He turned and looked at Ashlee. "Yeah, all right. You're great in the sack, Ashlee, but I want more than a good roll in the hay if I'm risking jail time."

She eyed him carefully in the early morning twilight. *I need him to get out of here. Once we're in Mexico, I'll have to rethink keeping him around. I don't need another man whose ego needs constant bolstering.*

Lowering her eyes coyly, she employed her little girl voice. "You're right. I've been very unappreciative. I promise I'll try harder to make this a team effort. When we get to Mexico, maybe we can relax a little and enjoy ourselves."

She took a step in Kurt's direction. When he didn't move, she reached her hand around his neck and drew him to her. With her lips brushing against his ear, she whispered, "I'm sorry, really I am."

She moved her mouth to his and gently kissed him, letting her soft lips linger on his. She felt his growing response as she slowly caressed his lips with her tongue. He groaned and pulled her body to his, slipping them both into darkness behind a parked van. He pressed against her, emphasizing his need as she moved her hand to his crotch and began slowly stroking the bulge covered by the khaki material of his uniform. A low animal sound escaped his lips, rumbling from deep inside his chest. He unbuttoned her uniform shirt and slid his hand into the opening under the lace bra, cupping her breast in his warm palm. He wandered into the warmth of her eager mouth, ringing her soft lips with his tongue.

Ashlee felt herself slipping into the sensations Kurt was stirring. His tongue tickled her lips and sent shivers up her spine, and his warm palm on her breast was comforting. He moved his thumb over the nipple, raising the baby soft skin to a hard sensitive point. Kurt slowly released his mouth from Ashlee's and, lightly trailing his tongue over her chin and down her smooth white neck, found her hardened nipple with his eager tongue. He popped the prize into his mouth gently flicking the tip. Ashlee moaned and squirmed muttering something incomprehensible and low. Kurt covered the nipple and sucked hard. Ashlee sighed, giving in to the urgings of her body, as Kurt's tongue danced little circular motions around her hardened bud sending waves of pleasure up her spine. She pushed her body against Kurt's, sliding his knee between her legs and grinding seductively.

Kurt let his hand slide under her waistband, slipping into the wetness between her legs, producing a low, animal sound from her. She pushed against him, reaching down to undo her trousers.

"No, don't." Kurt slipped his hand out of her pants.

"What? What do you mean?" Ashlee stared at him as he straightened himself. He stood looking down at her. Her breast was exposed and she was flushed. She'd managed to unbutton her pants, and the wig was slightly askew on her head.

"You'd better get dressed if we're going to make the flight on time." His amused expression was barely visible in the early morning light.

"What are you trying to do to me, Kurt Lee?" She scrambled to put herself together as Kurt started toward the terminal.

He stopped and turned to face her. "Two can play this game, Ashlee. Don't forget… you need me."

Ashlee sputtered, "You asshole!"

Kurt smirked. "You'd better get a move on or we'll miss our plane." He strode away.

Fingers shaking, Ashlee buttoned her trousers and shirt. She had to run to catch Kurt.

Grabbing his arm and jerking him around to face her, she spat out, "Don't you *ever* do that to me again."

He lowered his face to hers and stared directly into her eyes. "You have just been handed a major dose of 'Ashlee'. Don't think you can play me again. Now, for us to make it through without getting caught and going to jail, you're going to have to let me take the lead. I've arranged a story that will get us past the security checks and on the plane with our pistols. You need to play the role of the short silent type. Can you handle that?"

Clenching her teeth, Ashlee nodded.

Kurt reached toward her face and she caught his hand midair.

"Just what the hell are you doing?" She glared at him.

"Your wig is crooked. I was going to straighten it but that's okay. It's up to you if this is easy or hard."

She turned and straightened the wayward hairpiece, using the windows of a parked car as a mirror. She turned to Kurt. "This all right?"

"Fine. Now let's get the hell out of here." He moved toward the terminal, setting a rapid pace. He walked up to the first security guard he spotted and asked directions to the airport security offices.

"What for?" the guard said.

Kurt pulled his police shield from his pocket and flashed it. "Police matter."

"All right. Follow me." The guard grumbled as he led the pair through the main terminal, past specialty shops and restaurants. Halfway down the main thoroughfare, he turned left and disappeared.

Kurt and Ashlee quickened their pace and turned where they'd last seen him. They spotted him standing at the bottom of a gated staircase.

"Wait here." He unlocked the gate and, bounding up the steps, stood in front of a door at the top. He pushed a button and a muffled voice answered. After a brief conversation, he descended the stairs and, pointing to the top, he let them in the gate.

"Up on the right is a door. Push the button to the left and someone will buzz you in." He glared as he ushered the two past and closed the gate behind them.

"Isn't he the picture of sweetness and light?" Ashlee said.

Kurt shot her a dirty look. "Knock it off."

They followed his instructions and were admitted to an office overlooking the promenade of the airport. Windows looked down upon shops and cafes on one side, while the opposite side of the office looked over the tarmac of the airport. It was an impressive view. At the front desk sat a buxom blonde wearing the steel blue and crimson security uniform of the airport. She gave the pair in front of her the once over. "What can I do for you?"

"I need to speak to your officer in charge." Kurt straightened and peered down his nose at her.

A frown began to form on the secretary's face. "If you want to see the Captain, you'll have to tell me why."

Kurt gritted his teeth. "I'm following up on a warrant for a fugitive who escaped custody. The fugitive is armed and dangerous, and we believe she'll be fleeing the country from this airport. Will that work for you?"

The secretary picked up the phone. "Yeah, some sheriffs out here have lost a fugitive and need our help to find her. Sure. No problem." She hung up the phone and looked at the pair in front of her desk. She pointed at the only other door within the office.

"Through that door."

"Thank you," Kurt said.

"No problem."

Behind a government gray desk sat a lanky man whose once ebony hair was now streaked with silver. He motioned for the two to take a seat. Kurt noted the razor sharp creases in the captain's shirt. He wore the crew cut of a military man, and sat ramrod straight in his chair. The nameplate at the front of the desk was engraved Captain Robert Whitehead (USMC, Ret.).

"What can I do for you, Sheriff?" The chair squeaked as he leaned back.

Kurt set his briefcase on the desk and snapped open the lid. He pulled out an envelope, turned to Ashlee and, handing it to her, asked, "Please double check the facts for me."

She pulled the papers from inside. On Oakdale Police Department letterhead was a warrant naming Ashlee Anderson as an armed and dangerous fugitive from justice, who had escaped custody where she'd been held, pending trial, for attempted murder. Ashlee held the papers, perusing them; then she nodded affirmatively and handed the paperwork to Kurt who slid it toward the security officer for inspection.

Captain Whitehead picked up the papers and read the warrant. He looked over the top of the paperwork. "What has this got to do with my office?" He lifted one eyebrow.

Kurt cleared his throat. "Well, sir, we were hoping you would help expedite our passage to our flight. We have our weapons and need to check them through to the cockpit safe. We also need to pass your security inconspicuously so as not to arouse attention. Ashlee Anderson is good at blending in to the surrounding crowd and avoiding detection, and we'd like to have every opportunity to capture her. We also need to ask you to contact the authorities at Cancun, Mexico City and Mazatlán, so our arrival will be as trouble free as possible."

Captain Whitehead leaned forward and placed his elbows on his desk. "Why didn't your Captain complete this before you left?"

Kurt shifted in his chair and glanced sidelong at Ashlee.

"Ashlee Anderson was our captain until about a month ago. At that time, she was picked up on the attempted murder charge. When she escaped twenty-four hours ago, we had to scramble to get the warrant issued and move out before her trail became cold. We're really a small town force and this kind of international chase is something we haven't encountered before. Will you give us a hand?"

Captain Whitehead picked up a pencil and began tapping the eraser end on the desk.

Ashlee gripped the arms of the chair. The tapping was making her very nervous, and she was resisting the urge to reach over and snap the pencil in two.

"All right. I'll do what I can to simplify the security process at this end. I'll give a call to the airports in Mexico and let them know of your hunt, but once you're down there you're pretty much on your own. Do you have a pistol case for your weapons?"

Kurt reached into the briefcase and pulled out a black box which he opened on the captain's desk. He stood up, snapped open the leather strap from the pistol he carried and pulled the weapon out. He opened the chamber, emptied the bullets on the desk and, in a display reminiscent of his days in the police academy, dismantled his sidearm in less than a minute, handing the pieces to the captain. He turned to Ashlee.

"Officer Madison, if you please."

He motioned her to follow his example. Feeling sweat begin to trickle between her breasts, Ashlee stood. She straightened to attention and replied to Kurt.

"Officer Lee, I'm not thrilled with the idea of surrendering my weapon to anyone."

"I understand," Kurt's face was beginning to flush, "but with all the heightened security from September eleventh, we have to set an example and follow the rules like everyone else."

Ashlee stood for a moment, watching the color flood Kurt's face. Her steel blue eyes glittered with malevolence. She unsnapped the leather strap and handed the weapon to Kurt.

"You hand it to the Captain. Then when all is said and done, I can honestly say I surrendered my weapon to you."

Kurt snatched the gun out of her hands and, quickly dismantling it, pushed the pieces to the captain. The captain inspected each of the weapons, writing down the serial numbers stamped on the receiver of each automatic. He placed the pieces into the foam-lined box, closing and locking the lid.

"What time is your flight?" Captain Whitehead stood and picked up the weapon box from the desk.

Kurt glanced at his watch. "It leaves in about forty-five minutes."

"Then we'd better get moving. It'll take us at least twenty minutes to get to the gate and get you on the plane."

Filing past the blonde secretary and down the steps, the Captain locked the security gate and quick stepped past the security points directly to the boarding ramp. Stopping to speak with the airline employee at the desk, he checked the pair through and walked them on to the waiting plane. The flight attendant escorted them to their seats in business class where they settled. Kurt sat on the aisle and watched as the captain knocked on the cockpit door. A pilot appeared and a clipped conversation ensued with the captain pointing to Kurt. The pilot nodded his acknowledgement of Kurt, took the black box and closed the cockpit door.

The captain gave a short salute and disappeared from the plane. Kurt leaned back in the seat and smiled at Ashlee. "Looks like we're on our way."

"Until this plane leave U.S. airspace and lands in Mexico, we're not safe. Don't get complacent." She leaned her head against the seatback and closed her eyes. A jolt and the sensation of motion brought her head forward and she opened her eyes. She peered out the window to see the building slowly disappearing from her view.

~ * ~

Captain Whitehead watched the plane being pushed away from the terminal. *Every piece of paper they handed me was in order.* He scratched the palm of his left hand unconsciously. *Everything had signatures, and they surrendered their weapons without a fight, but something just doesn't feel right.*

He monitored the plane as it taxied down the runway, gaining speed and finally lifting into the air. *Oh, well, Mexico's problem now.*

~ * ~

Ashlee watched the land drop from view. "Captain Whitehead didn't buy everything we fed him, you know?"

She looked at Kurt. He was strapped into his seat, his head lolling back and he was softly snoring. *You are an idiot, Kurt Lee, but a useful idiot. If I didn't need you, I'd be tempted to push you out the emergency hatch.*

She leaned against the seat and let the exhaustion draw her eyelids down. A smile spread across her face as she pictured Kurt falling through the sky. *No one controls me—no one.*

# Fourteen

Corey burrowed into the dangerously high stacks of paperwork piled on his desk with the tenacity of a badger.

"What are you searching for?" Riona asked. She was sitting in one of the visitor chairs across from him watching his performance.

"Remember I told you I thought I knew who the inside person was with Ashlee?"

She nodded.

"Well, an innocuous piece of paper crossed my desk about a week ago and, at the time, I thought it was odd and out of place. However, with the wedding and everything I forgot about it."

"Why did it bother you?"

She was glancing at her watch. It was nearly nine a.m. and Ashlee Anderson had an eight hour start on them. They needed to get moving if they had any chance to catch her.

Corey stuck his hand into a pile of paperwork and extracted one sheet. He turned the paper right side up. The corners of his mouth began to form a smile. "Got you, you little bastard."

"What is it?"

"Proof that will prove my conspiracy theory. So much in this case seemed coincidental, but lately it had become too coincidental. All the signs pointed back to this office, and one officer in particular. This last request put the nail in his coffin."

Riona was sitting on the edge of her seat leaning toward Corey, watching his face change as he put the pieces of the puzzle together.

"Okay, give. Who is it?" she said.

Corey turned the paper face down on the desk and leaned back in his chair ignoring the protest of the springs. He looked into her chocolate brown eyes and spoke slowly and evenly. "Nothing we discuss here is to be printed until I give you the go ahead."

"Man, you can't hobble me like this," Riona started.

"We made an agreement at the hospital, remember?"

"Yeah, but…"

"No buts. It's essential we keep this under wraps until we have Ashlee and the officer under arrest. Now, do I have your solemn promise not to call in, print, write, or hint about this to your editor or any other news agency on the face of this planet?" Corey leaned forward, his chair squeaking and complaining.

"Man, you're killing my career here. Okay, okay. I'll keep a lid on this information until I get the go ahead from you, but you owe me big time, buster." She slumped against the back of her chair, crossing her arms and affecting a pout worthy of Ashlee Anderson.

Corey turned over the piece of paper he had in front of him and slid it toward Riona. "This form is an official extradition request," he said.

"And?"

"It was sent through the system two weeks ago by an officer who is technically a paper pusher and shouldn't have need for an extradition order for any reason. He's been hovering around the edges of this case since the beginning. I've had a suspicion he might be involved, but no evidence to back up my gut feeling. He followed Ashlee like a dog in heat during high school and was furious when she went off to college and married Justin Anderson. I guess he was never far out of the picture."

"Corey?"

"Yeah?"

"This is all well and good, but if we don't get moving to try and find these guys, we'll lose any trail they may have left. We have no clue where they were headed. It's a pretty big world out there," she said.

"There is one good thing about an extradition order—it requires a destination. They're headed to Mexico." Corey grinned.

"Great. Do you know how many thousands of miles there are in Mexico?" Riona blew an exasperated breath through her lips.

Corey watched her purse her lips and felt himself stirring. *Not now.* "I'm pretty sure they'd have to go through airport security if they want to carry any weapons, in which case, they'll need to state a definite landing destination. Mexico's laws about carrying weapons are completely different than the U.S. They'll have to contact the local *Federalés* and sweet talk them so they can carry their side arms." Corey's face flushed with excitement.

"Then, let's get the hell out of here."

"You don't have any luggage. How do you expect to change clothes or brush your teeth or anything?" he asked.

Riona reached into her vest pocket and pulled out two items. She flipped open her passport and wallet exposing a row of credit cards.

"Credit."

"Oh, yeah."

She reached into the opposite inner vest pocket and produced a travel toothbrush set. "Like a boy scout, I'm always prepared." She grinned at the detective.

Shaking his head and smiling, Corey picked up the phone. "Sarge? I'm going to be out of the office for a couple of weeks on a case I'm following. Let the captain know, will you? If anything important comes up… well, just in case it does, have Donnie White handle it until I get back. Out in the impound lot is an emerald Harley Davidson. Please put a tarp over it and keep a close eye on it. If anything happens, I'll let you explain to the tall redhead that owns it. That's what I thought. I'll check in periodically to let you know what's happening." He stood up and looked at Riona. "Ready?"

She stood, pushing the chair back. "Let's go. Where do we start?"

"I'm pretty sure they flew out of Dulles since it's the only airport within driving distance. We can start there and ask the lot attendants to keep an eye on any vehicle that seems out of place. However, if it was me, I'd park in long term parking because nobody will check there for at least a month. After that, we need to visit airport security. If they haven't checked in, maybe the surveillance cameras got a picture of them at their departure gate."

"I sure hope so, because the longer we sit around trying to track down leads, the farther away they get," she said.

The detective exited his office and moved briskly toward the rear of the building with the reporter following closely behind him. He headed to an unmarked but obvious police cruiser.

Opening the door, he waited for his passenger. Riona critically surveyed the vehicle. "A little obvious, isn't it?" she asked.

"And my truck isn't?" Corey raised an eyebrow.

"Point well taken," she said.

He walked around the front of the vehicle and crawled into the driver's seat. He spent the first five minutes completing a required safety check then maneuvered the squad car out of the parking lot to the city streets. The gazebo in the town square sparkled in the morning light with droplets of water left by the sprinklers. The heat of the day hadn't wilted the overhanging trees shading the park or grass yet, and the sky was a shimmering crystal blue. They moved past the quaint century old buildings, respecting the posted twenty-five miles per hour signs. At the edge of town, Corey gave the big car a burst of gas. Cruising at speed, the couple silently mused.

Riona spoke first. "This is really eating you alive. Do you want to share?"

Corey shifted his bulk and cleared his throat. "This is going to be a long trip and maybe after a day or two I'll feel more talkative, but right now—I… I need to regroup. I have a very good friend whose life and happiness is in danger as long as Ashlee Anderson is free. I feel this slipup is my responsibility. I should have known—should have seen the signs." Corey pounded the steering wheel with his fist.

Riona bit her lower lip. She knew only too well what Corey was feeling. She'd lived through the same nightmare.

~ * ~

Captain Martichev stayed close to the buildings, moving in the shadows. Cinching the belt on his greatcoat tighter, he ducked into the mud hovel he used as his sleeping quarters and office. The hovel was the only structure in the village whose windows were still intact. The Mulah of the village had fled this home before the Russians entered the outskirts of the town.

Pushing the door closed against the howling wind, he moved to the coarse wood table that served as desk and dinner table. He touched the flame of his lighter to the half used candle, watching as the blaze flickered in the breeze creeping through the cracks around the splintered, desiccated windowsills.

He tossed the greatcoat over the back of the wooden chair placed next to his bed. Dropping to the cot, he fought the feeling of nausea washing over him. *How could I be excited by kissing another man? I've been in this cursed Muslim country too long.*

A gust of wind snuffed the light from the candle. Captain Martichev sighed. *May as well sleep. Tomorrow the colonel will be here, and I should be sharp. If he's happy with my success here, he might send me home.* He swung his booted legs onto the cot and covered himself with the down filled sleeping bag and a blanket. Sleep overtook him.

~ * ~

"Captain, Captain."

The sergeant's voice broke through the dark vacuum of sleep. The captain stirred, his eyes flickered. The taste of sour liquor clung to his tongue. Opening his eyes, he squinted against a shaft of sunlight streaming through a space between the windows. His groan echoed off the bare walls as his fuzzy brain tried to grasp where he was. *Oh, yes. The colonel will show up, and issue orders about things which he has little or no knowledge.*

He moved the covers aside and pushed to a seated position, running his hand over his blonde crew cut.

The sergeant handed him a steaming cup of chai; a local concoction of strong tea with lots of sugar, and cream—when available. The captain grasped the small steaming cup in his hands and lifted it to his lips. He blew across the top of the tea then gingerly sipped the scalding liquid.

"Damn, that's hot." He sucked in cool air over his now burnt lips.

"That's the idea of putting it over a fire," said the sergeant.

André threw a dirty look at the sergeant and stood up to stretch his limbs.

"By the way, there's a reporter waiting out front to see you."

André froze. His arms ached with remembrance. "I'm busy. Tell him to make an appointment for another time."

The door flung open and Colonel Popov swept into the room. "Captain Martichev. We must keep up our good relations with the press." He turned and waved the reporter into the room.

"Come in, come in. What can we do for you?"

The reporter entered hesitantly, squinting against the dark interior. "I wish to speak with the Captain."

Colonel Popov planted his feet and, raising an eyebrow, turned in the captain's direction. "Well, André?"

The captain rose from his cot and indicated to the reporter to sit at the table. "What can I do for you?"

"I wanted to thank you for your escort last evening. I would certainly have been robbed or worse had you not seen to my safety."

"How do you know it was I who helped you?"

"The clerk at the front desk of my hotel recognized you."

"Oh. Well, you're welcome. If you're going to survive in this country, you need to smarten up. I would've thought they'd have educated you before you left wherever it is you call home."

André watched the reporter through hooded eyes as he spoke. The reporter stiffened with André's insult. Reaching into his hip pocket, he pulled out a cigarette pack and offered one to the captain, who took the western smoke and accepted a light.

"Captain?"

"Martichev."

"Martichev, I'm Irish by birth and work for an international news organization."

Andre listened dispassionately as the reporter listed his experience and knowledge of the country they both occupied. He explained that the previous night had been a release of the pent up frustrations of trying to relay news from a Muslim country which still used camels as their main transportation. The Captain watched the reporter light another cigarette off the previous one. Something about the way he handled the cigarette triggered his memory. *That's it! This reporter is a woman masquerading as a man!*

~ * ~

Riona smiled at the memory and a shiver spider-webbed over her skin. She pictured the handsome blonde captain in his great coat, sporting his perpetual day old stubble. He'd seen through her carefully planned disguise. The soul penetrating intensity with which his gray eyes stared into hers as he snubbed out his cigarette had further dried her mouth that morning.

Her hand went to her throat and she ran a finger over the unicorn.

"Everything okay?" Corey glanced sidelong at his passenger.

"Yeah, fine."

"I'm going to park near the terminal and head for the airport security office. They'll have declared a destination if they wanted any chance of taking their weapons with them. Then we'll have to purchase tickets and follow them. With any luck, we might actually be able to catch them in the next twenty-four to forty-eight hours."

Corey parked the police cruiser in the area marked: Official Vehicles Only. After securing the auto, he and Riona walked inside the airport terminal. A quick scan of the busy ticket counter area provided Corey with the knowledge that a uniformed security officer manned each corridor to the docking area. He chose the closest guard and asked to be taken to the terminal security office. The guard grunted and indicated for them to follow as he led them down the main shopping and eating area of the airport. He stopped at the bottom of a gated flight of stairs and unlocked the gate. He went up the stairs and, after a brief consultation, came back down again and led Corey and Riona up to the security offices.

A petite redhead in uniform briskly tapped the keys of a computer. She turned and greeted the duo.

"May I help you?"

"I'd like to speak to the Officer in charge," Corey said.

"Do you have an appointment?" she asked.

"No, but it's imperative I speak to him or her immediately. Time is of the essence here," Corey replied.

"Well, I would need to see some identification before we go any further."

Corey pulled his badge wallet from his overcoat inner pocket and, flipping it open, he laid it on the desk for her to view. She raked over the badge and security card with his picture.

"You look better in person," she commented.

"Thanks," he said.

"What about her?" She nodded in Riona's direction.

Imitating Corey's movements, Riona offered her newspaper ID.

The little redhead looked at the ID and raised her eyebrows. "The press?"

Corey sighed, replaced his badge in his pocket, and replied, "Long story, but I'll vouch for her."

"Well, Detective, I'll have to trust you on this. I'll need to have a little more information before I talk with the Officer in charge. What is so important you couldn't call and make an appointment?"

"I believe two armed felons posing as police officers from my station came through here earlier today and may have checked in with your office. I'd like to see if my suspicions are justified."

Leaning back in her chair and crossing her arms over her chest, the redhead hotly replied, "That's impossible."

"Please allow me a few minutes of the Officer's time so I can straighten this out and prove or disprove my suspicions."

The receptionist didn't budge for a full minute. Finally, she sighed and picked up the phone.

"Yeah, Eddy? I really hate to disturb you but there's a Detective out here who would like to talk with you. Yeah, it seems pretty important. Okay." She pointed to a door. "Go on in. He said you have five minutes."

Captain Edward Lynnes didn't need to work. His army retirement was sufficient to cover his needs, but at fifty years old he wasn't ready to sit on the porch in a rocking chair. When his friend Bob Whitehead had called and suggested he come to work at the airport, Ed jumped at the chance.

He eyed the unusual pair entering his office. The sheriff stood over six and a half feet tall, could've afforded to lose about fifty pounds, and looked serious enough to scare small children. His companion, a six-foot tall redhead with serious brown eyes who introduced herself as a reporter, looked him in the eye as they walked in and took the seats he offered. Her squared shoulders and set jaw convinced him she was as serious about their business as the detective. When he'd stood to shake hands with the two, her hand was as calloused as the detective's and her handshake as firm. Ed found himself glancing at her as the sheriff spoke. She intrigued his curiosity. She wasn't wearing a sheriff's uniform but appeared to be on the same quest as the detective.

"Thank you, Captain, for seeing us. We have a situation we need to move on as quickly as possible. I believe one of my officers, and a fugitive posing as an officer, might have passed through your office earlier this morning. I was hoping they'd given you a specific destination," Corey said.

"I'll check our log to see if anything unusual happened on the last couple of shifts."

He placed a quick call to the receptionist who brought the daily log into the office. The silence in his office was broken by the hum of the air conditioner and crinkle of pages as he skimmed the report.

"I think this is what you might be looking for." He read the entry aloud: "'*Five fifteen a.m. Two officers from Oakdale, VA, came into the office—Kurt Lee and Elaine Madison. Asked to have side arms checked through this office; presented a fugitive warrant for one Ashlee Anderson, destination Mexico. The night Captain checked their broken down weapons, and secured them into a black carrying case provided by Officer Lee. The captain escorted them on the plane, checked the weapons into the cockpit lockbox and made sure they found their seats. Plane left the tarmac at five forty-five a.m.*'" The captain glanced at his wristwatch.

"The plane should have landed in Mexico about an hour ago. If it's any consolation, we've developed a very close working relationship with the Mexican authorities. They'll have to check in with customs, then the Mexican *Federalés*—police, especially if they want to keep their weapons. We might be able to call and have them stopped if you want."

Corey and Riona exchanged glances.

"Thanks, but I'm afraid these two are desperate enough to harm anyone who tries to get in their way. If you'll check us through and help get us on the next flight to Cancun that would be more than enough help." Corey pulled his weapon and placed it on the desk in front of the captain.

The captain looked at Corey's weapon and up at Corey.

"Exactly what's going on, detective?" the captain asked.

He pulled the revolver to him, released the clip into his palm and placed it on the desk. He then removed the bullet from the chamber, and proceeding to field strip the weapon, arranged the pieces into a carrying case the detective had placed on the desk.

"I—we—believe the woman passing herself off as Elaine Madison is, in reality, Ashlee Anderson. She has used her wiles to enlist Officer Lee into helping her escape from custody. She caused herself enough injury to require stitches and an overnight stay in the hospital, where she incapacitated the female officer guarding her and adopted the officer's identity, then fled with Officer Lee."

Riona's cell phone buzzed. "Excuse me. I'll take this in the reception area." She walked into the outer room.

The captain leaned toward Corey. "What's with the reporter?"

Corey leaned back in his chair, the corners of his mouth turning up slightly, and sighed. "It's a really long story but let's just say, I made a deal with the devil."

Ed watched as the statuesque woman reentered the room. He smirked at Corey. "I think you may have beaten him at his own game."

"Anything important?" Corey turned to Riona as she slipped into the chair next to him.

"Just my editor," she said.

Corey stiffened in his chair. "You didn't say anything, did you?"

"I told him I would guarantee a Pulitzer for the paper in a week or so, but now he needed to trust my instincts and let me do what I do best—get the story. He'll leave me alone."

Captain Lynnes cleared his throat. "I think you folks might have a bit of a problem." He tapped the log which lay open on his desk.

"How's that?" Corey asked.

"Well, as I told you, the two officers stated they were headed to Mexico. Unfortunately, they gave three locations—Cancun, Mexico City and Mazatlán."

Corey groaned and lowered his head to his hands.

"I've got two weeks to try and track these fugitives down and bring them back to face justice."

"I guess this is where I come in." Riona crossed her leg over her knee. "Once we're in the air, I can place a few calls to some people I know in Mexico and help narrow our search field."

Corey turned to her. "Am I gonna regret this?"

"Quite possibly, but do you have a better solution?"

"Not at the present time," Corey said.

"When is the next flight to Cancun?" Corey asked the captain.

Captain Lynnes consulted with the receptionist who brought in a flight schedule. After briefly glancing at the timetable, he handed the schedule to Corey.

"Looks like you've got a couple of hours to kill. You might want to take advantage of some of the airport restaurants since it's likely to be a while until you eat again."

"Again? I haven't eaten since last night." Riona rose from her seat. "Let's get some food. I'm starving." She strode toward the door. "We'll be back in time for you to check us through, Captain."

The look of surprise on the detective's face told the captain the reporter had trumped him. Detective Williams wrestled himself out of the chair and followed the tall redhead.

"Why are you running?" Corey puffed.

"We need to set a plan for ourselves, and we don't need to include every law officer on the east coast."

Riona turned into a dimly lit café. The sign outside the cafe boasted seventy-five different types of coffee. *Great. Just what I need is coffee. I'll be awake for a month.*

Corey stopped inside the doorway. He squinted to make out the tables, and follow the rhythmic stride of Riona.

She turned. "Are you coming?"

"I'm trying to see," he was beginning to make out the tables and chairs. "I wanted some color this summer but black and blue wasn't my first choice."

Riona had settled herself at a table in the darkest corner of the room. Corey slowly inched his way toward the table choosing to sit in a chair opposite her.

"You're acting awfully skittish. What's up?" He grabbed the menu from the center holder.

"I can't explain it yet, but I've got a really bad feeling about this security guy. He asks too many questions."

"Riona, it's his job. Maybe you'll feel different after you have something to eat. I know I will." Corey's eyes swept over the menu.

Riona flipped open the menu in front of her.

A young man, sporting green and blonde hair, languidly approached the table. Riona openly stared at the gold ring sticking out from the end of the young man's eyebrow. A matching earring graced his left ear. Tall and thin, his black attire did little to warm his appearance.

"Ready to order?" He licked the end of his pencil and poised it over his pad.

Riona shuddered when she noticed the stud in the young man's tongue.

"I'll have the breakfast special with ice tea." Riona put the menu back in the holder.

"Make mine the same, with pork chops and plain coffee." Corey said.

The waiter rolled his eyes toward the ceiling and wandered off to the kitchen to place the orders.

When their meals arrived, a quiet settled over the table as the two dug into their food.

Riona leaned against the back of her chair and sipped her iced tea. She eyed the man she was accompanying. His large frame overwhelmed the chair in which he sat. She watched him cut his pork chop into small bites and carefully chew each one, wiping his mouth with his napkin afterward. Her gaze swept over his ruddy complexion and red brown hair. His hazel eyes lifted to meet hers.

"What? What did I do?" he asked.

Riona shook her head. "Nothing." *I'm not ready to let you know I'm beginning to get attached to that face—not yet.*

He nodded when the sullen waiter asked if he wanted more coffee.

"We've got about an hour before we board." Corey glanced at his watch.

"Let's stay here and head back to the security office as soon as we're both done, okay?" she said.

"Good idea."

"You've asked me—twice I might add—how I got to know Justin and Diane. It's my turn to ask. I know you said you knew Justin in high school, but how did you meet them?" Riona absently turned the spoon in her iced tea glass.

Corey took a sip of his coffee, allowing the aroma of the strong black brew to caress his nose. He leaned back in his chair and picked up a spoon from the table. Placing the utensil between his thumb and forefinger he stroked the smoothness like a worry stone, letting the cool sensation of the metal sooth his frazzled nerves. Riona made his palms sweat and groin react. Clearing his throat, he began.

"Justin and I attended school together since his freshman and my sophomore year. He had an older brother who was a gifted basketball player and two years his senior. Justin chose to play football and was good, but a little small, so I took it on myself to look after him. We became friends. The year his family was killed our friendship became important to both of us. I spent a lot of time with him and his sister at his grandmother's home, where they were living. We watched each other's back in those days. Frankly, I thought he'd lost his mind when he came back from college all starry eyed and announced he was marrying Ashlee. He was my friend and I kept my mouth shut. If nothing else, he got Briana, his daughter, out of the deal and, Lord knows, I love that little girl. When he started receiving threats, I knew it had to be Ashlee. She didn't want him, but she sure didn't want anyone else to have him either. I was pleased when Diane moved into town and he decided to pursue her. She's strong and didn't wimp out under Ashlee's pressure.

"One of the greatest pleasures of my career, so far, has been locking up Ashlee's lover and watching as she was fingerprinted, photographed, and locked in a cell herself. I had this uncomfortable feeling every night she was incarcerated that I was going to get a call at home telling me she'd escaped. That's why I was so adamant about having a guard on her cell and the room at the hospital. I knew she'd find a way to get out. One thing about Ashlee remains constant, and that's her deviousness. I'm determined to see her spend as much time as possible behind bars." Corey smacked the spoon on the table.

Riona jumped. She'd watched him become more animated the longer he spoke. His face flushed and his eyes twinkled and darted as he talked about his friend. She could sense another story emerging. She wanted to find out about this man who cared so deeply for his friends. He fostered an illusion of softness and, yes, even ignorance that was just—an illusion. She'd felt a keen edge and hardness in his speech. "You're taking this rather personally, aren't you?"

"Wouldn't you? We're talking about my good friend. Even if a total stranger was involved, murder is nothing to take lightly. I want to see Ashlee in jail, where she belongs."

The airport public address system announced the flight to Cancun was boarding on concourse F, gate fifteen.

"I guess that's us." Corey started to rise.

"No."

He stopped and stared at Riona.

"Why not?"

"Think about it. If you were Ashlee, what would be your most likely plan of action? Smoke and mirrors? She's going to try and send us on a wild goose chase. If I were in her position, I'd come up with names of places spread so far apart that even using the phone system would make tracking me down impossible. What were the destinations they told security?"

"Cancun, Mexico City and, what did he say? Oh yeah, Mazatlán," Corey answered.

"Okay, for the time being, let's think like Ashlee. Cancun is too obvious. It's a direct flight from D.C. and while it provides a lot of entertainment, there's no work but the tourist businesses. It's also fairly expensive. Mexico City seems all wrong for Ashlee. It's too—Mexican, too ethnic. There are lots of places for an enterprising American to work but the American community in Mexico City is very exclusive. Ashlee doesn't have enough money or class to fit into that group. I think we can pretty well conclude she'd head for Mazatlán. It's as far from Oakdale as she can get, on the ocean, and the living is very affordable outside the city limits. She'd be able to rent a small bungalow for years on a very small amount. I suspect she may have squirreled away some money in a Mexican bank and will be heading for it to tide her over. Does that sound like the Ashlee you know?"

Corey nodded. He had to agree with Riona's assessment of the situation. Ashlee Anderson always did what was best for Ashlee Anderson. She'd do whatever it took to keep herself out of jail. He was certain Kurt Lee had no idea what was happening and was in more danger than he realized.

## Fifteen

Kurt stared at Ashlee's voluptuous breasts rising and falling as she slept. Her black lashes fluttered against her pale cheeks as she dropped into a deep slumber, her pouty lips pursing with each breath. The bandage covering her stitches seemed out of place on her otherwise perfect face. He cautiously raised a finger and caressed her porcelain cheek. The velvety sensation sent his mind racing, and other body parts reacting.

"If you touch me again, I'll break your finger and the attached arm," Ashlee growled.

Kurt jumped and jerked his hand away from her face. He turned and stared at the woman next to him feigning sleep.

"I—I thought you were asleep," he stuttered.

"I know you did. If you do that again, you'll pull back a stump. Are we clear?" Ashlee hadn't opened her eyes while she spoke.

Kurt was in this up to his neck. Ashlee's heavy breathing and panting over him had ceased once they had flown over the U.S./Mexican border and he wasn't about to get himself locked up in a Mexican jail on her account. He patted the arrest papers in his pocket. If she got to be too much of a smart ass, he'd turn her in and take the glory for himself. After all, who'd they believe, Ashlee the criminal or Kurt the law officer?

He settled against the seat and smiled.

~ * ~

Three hours later, the intercom crackled and a voice announced the plane's arrival in Cancun within the next twenty minutes. The passengers were instructed to take their seats and place the backs and trays in the upright positions. The message was then repeated in Spanish.

Kurt stretched and contemplated waking Ashlee, until she stirred. She stretched each of her limbs slowly and carefully, reminding Kurt of a cat—cuddly in appearance but armed with deadly fangs and claws.

"We've got about twenty minutes before touchdown." Kurt tightened his seatbelt.

"I'm dying for a cigarette. Hopefully we'll have time to find a coffee shop that serves a decent cappuccino." Ashlee wiggled in her seat and muttered to Kurt. "These damned uniforms are uncomfortable as well as ugly."

He smirked. "But you have to admit, they open a lot of doors."

Ashlee narrowed her eyes and measured her words carefully. "You have helped get me to this point, but be assured I would have found a way out—with or without you." She gazed out the window at the passing landscape below.

The 'Fasten Seatbelt' sign lit up, and the flight attendants began to move quickly up and down the aisles picking up glasses and other leftovers. They scurried to the back of the plane and strapped themselves in their jump seats for the landing. The plane shuddered slightly when the wheels lowered and locked into the landing position. Ashlee watched the flaps lower and listened as their motors whined over the jet noise. Lush peninsula vegetation rushed to meet the speeding mechanical bird. Distracting her from the plane was a red-sailed para-glider, its occupant tied by a thin white line to the sleek white boat chiseling a path through the turquoise water.

Ashlee's hand slid to her forehead, her slender fingers finding the throbbing stitches near her hairline. She licked her lips and peered more intensely at the white sand strip below, sprinkled with tiny dots of color. Her mouth turned up at the corners as she thought of her daughter Briana.

*She'd say how much it looks like an ice cream cone with sprinkles. I really need to get in contact with her when we land. There must be a way I can arrange for her to join me.*

"What are you smiling about?" Kurt asked.

Ashlee's smile faded.

"Nothing. I need to find a phone when we touch down."

"Why?"

"Isn't it obvious? I need to make a phone call."

The plane bumped on the runway and immediately began to shudder as the pilot braked and powered down the engines. He taxied the craft to the gate, the engines whining as they slowed. Before the outer hatch door had opened, the aisles filled with passengers reaching to the overhead compartments for luggage. Kurt started to unsnap his seat belt when Ashlee grabbed his arm.

"Where are you going?" she asked.

"To the terminal," he said.

"Let everyone else get off first then we'll go."

"But—"

She glared at him. He leaned back and watched the variety of people jostling to escape the confines of the aluminum bird. When the last passenger had disembarked, Ashlee stood up, nudging Kurt with her knee until he rose, and moved into the aisle. She strode up and knocked on the cockpit door.

An officer in uniform stepped out.

"Yes, ma'am?"

"Yes, we'd like to disembark from the plane before it goes to its final destination in Mazatlán. However, we'd prefer to have our weapons with us. What are the regulations about carrying guns inside the terminal?"

"First, Officer Madison," the flight officer glanced at the nametag Ashlee wore over her pocket, "we're not leaving for Mazatlán for six hours. Secondly, the Mexican government frowns on non-Mexican police officers carrying guns unless absolutely necessary. We have to keep them locked up until your final destination; at which time, we'll escort you and the weapons to the *Federalés* Office to check in with all your paperwork."

"Oh," Ashlee pushed out her lower lip.

The officer shrugged and stepped back into the cockpit.

Not having succeeded in coercing the flight officer, she turned on her heel, stomped out of the plane and up the entry corridor. Kurt trailed behind, dreading the inevitable temper tantrum about to ensue.

Although it was still morning, Ashlee walked directly toward the first bar she spied. The only thought on her mind was getting a Bloody Mary and trying to find a way to contact Briana.

*Damn it. She's with Justin and that woman he married. Oh, well. When I settle here, I'll find a way to get my daughter back.*

She sat on a bar stool, facing the windows which looked out over the beach and ocean. The tall, dark bartender walked over and set a napkin in front of Ashlee and Kurt, who'd sat in the bar stool next to hers. The young bartender's smile revealed perfect white teeth against his tanned, handsome face.

"What can I get for you this morning?" His sumptuous brown eyes looked directly at Ashlee.

"You speak English," she said.

"Born in Brooklyn and raised in the good ole' US of A. You bet. What'll it be this morning?" he repeated.

"I need a Bloody Mary," Ashlee said.

He turned to Kurt. "And for you?"

"Coffee, black."

The bartender began preparing their requests.

Ashlee lit a cigarette and pulled the smoke deep into her lungs. Kurt watched as her shoulders slowly lowered and her body began to liquefy in the barstool.

"You feeling a little better?" he ventured.

"Yeah, I am. I really hate the new laws about not smoking on international flights. It sucks. I think maybe I might be a little hungry, too. Did you bring along the cash?"

"Yes. I took the card you gave me and withdrew as much as I could the week before we left. I didn't have any problem at the bank because I went to Donna Zeke's window each time and gave her some song and dance about this being for your mom who wasn't feeling well. She didn't bat an eye and handed it over. We have enough to last us for about a year if we budget carefully," Kurt said.

"Budget? I've got a certain standard of living, and I have no intention of changing it. My research showed I can live my lifestyle here in Mexico for about one quarter what it costs back home, if I go to the right place. Why do you think I chose to come here? It wasn't my love of Mexican food, that's for sure. So don't start in on me about budgeting. After all, it is my money. Now, I'm going to buy myself a decent meal and you're going to pay for it, without giving me a lecture, right?" Ashlee looked at Kurt dangerously.

"What would you like?" He was in no mood to argue.

When the bartender returned with their drinks, the two had decided on steak and eggs. They placed an order and sat in silence, watching the activity on the tarmac of the airport. The flawless blue sky provided a perfect backdrop for the silver planes swooping on to the runway. Logos from all over the world graced the tail sections of the planes ferrying into the arms of the concourses. When they'd finally stopped rolling, the tarmac took on the appearance of an anthill with workers; scurrying to fuel jets and to restock the silver birds for their flights to other destinations.

The busy world outside the window was a far cry from the mood inside the bar. Having finished their breakfast, Kurt and Ashlee sat absorbed in their own thoughts.

"What are we going to do for another five hours?" Ashlee asked.

"We could act like we're seriously looking for a fugitive," he replied.

"What do you mean?" she said.

Kurt pulled the sheaf of papers from his pocket and rifled through it. Stopping mid-way, he pulled a notebook size sheet out and shoved it toward Ashlee. She picked up the form and scrutinized the picture and printed information.

"Your organizational skills surprise me—a wanted poster with Elaine's picture on it. Very clever." She nodded her head in his direction.

"What we can do is make a big deal about going into all of the restaurants and small shops to show this around, asking if they've seen her. We'll cover our story we're searching for a fugitive." Kurt pulled the paper in front of him.

The bartender came over to the solitary couple.

"You guys doing okay?"

"Yeah, but I have a question." Ashlee leaned toward the young man, giving him a clear view of her womanly assets.

The bartender rose to the bait and leaned on the bar in front of her.

"Go ahead, beautiful." He flashed a dazzling white smile.

"Do most of the folks who work in the airport speak English or do most of them speak Spanish?" She leaned even closer to the young man.

"Most of the folks speak Spanish, why?"

He leaned so close Ashlee could smell the mint on his breath and the spicy cologne he wore.

"Well, I'm sure you noticed we're police…" she started.

"The uniforms gave it away," he smirked.

"…anyway," she dropped her eyes coyly and swept her lashes up to catch him gazing down the front of her blouse. "We need someone to help us in locating a fugitive we've been sent to recover. Could you recommend someone who'd be able to help us? I'm afraid we wouldn't be able to pay them in dollars but we might be able to work out some other agreement." Ashlee leaned closer, her lips brushing the bartender's. She sat back and batted her eyes innocently.

The bartender pulled back, his expression unclear. He cocked his head and looked directly into Ashlee's eyes. His tongue swept around his full lips, tasting where her mouth had lingered on his.

"If you can wait until two, I get off work and will be happy to offer my Spanish speaking services in your search." He licked his lips again, his mouth turning up in a smile.

Ashlee leaned as far over the bar as she could. She pulled him to her mouth and placed an urgent kiss on his lips. She slipped her tongue into his mouth and left a promise waiting.

Sitting back in her chair, she mouthed *thank you* to him. She picked up her empty glass. "Again?"

The young bartender nodded and moved to make her another drink.

"What was that all about?" Kurt's mouth was set in a grim line.

"That was about using what we have to get something, without using any of our cash. We now have an interpreter who won't hold back what's being said."

Ashlee lit another cigarette and blew the smoke in Kurt's face.

He coughed and fanned away the smoke.

"I need some fresh air." He got up and moved out of the bar. *Once we get to Mazatlan, I could take off and leave her conniving butt in the lurch. After all, I have all the money.* The thought comforted him as he strolled down the concourse.

The walk enabled Kurt to estimate how long it would take to talk with all of the airport personnel. They'd be able to accomplish their task in about two to three hours. Instead of sitting and watching Ashlee fawn over some young stud muffin, he'd be laying down a much needed smoke screen to back up the story they were trying to weave. He turned at the end of the concourse and walked back to the bar. Business was picking up as the flights started arriving faster. The young man Ashlee was trying to impress was too busy doing his job to be standing around ogling her. Kurt sat next to her.

"Where've you been?" She turned and fastened a cold stare on him.

"I've been reconnoitering the airport," he said.

"You've what?"

"I took a stroll to see how many places we'll need to stop once your friend gets off work and can help us," he explained.

"Why didn't you just say that? By the way," Ashlee held her hand out, palm up. "You need to hand over *my* money. I've worked too hard earning it and I won't be like some child asking for an allowance. Hand it over."

Kurt stared at her for a moment, not moving. His plan of freedom from Ashlee was evaporating in front of his eyes.

Lowering her voice and turning her icy blue eyes his direction, she growled, "Now."

He dug into his pocket and retrieved an envelope bulging with money. Placing the envelope on the bar, he reached in and pulled out a twenty.

Ashlee's eyes widened. "What makes you think you can do that?"

"I paid for breakfast and your drinks out of my pocket. You can pay your own way from this point forward." He slid the envelope to her. He opened his wallet and put the twenty inside.

She picked up the envelope, glancing around the room to see if they'd been observed, and shoved the bulging white wrapper inside her uniform shirt next to her body. Most of her adult life was represented in that container. From this point forward, she was holding on to the controls in her life. She slid back on the bar stool and observed her companion. He'd been fascinated with her since they were in high school and getting him to help with this escape had proven easy, but she sensed, from his recent outburst at the airport in D.C., he was changing his mind. She'd have to soften her stance until she was settled, then she would eliminate him from the picture. Until that time, she really did need him. She could fake anything including being a police woman, but Kurt was the real deal and would be able to talk with the local authorities to bolster their charade. She'd ride along for a little while longer. Ashlee jumped when the bartender touched her arm.

"Sorry. I'll clock out then we can start checking with everyone to see if they've seen your fugitive. Give me about ten minutes, okay?" The bartender smiled and disappeared through a door behind the bar.

Ashlee nodded. When the bartender had disappeared, she spoke.

"Tony will be back in about ten minutes. You'd better start acting like my partner and not my lover. Remember, we're here as a team looking for a fugitive," she said.

"Yeah, I'll be just fine. You made your plans crystal clear the moment we arrived in Mexico. I'll be professional and follow through until we reach our destination. At that point, you're on your own." Kurt stood and shook the cramps out of his legs.

Ashlee realized she needed to smooth things over or she'd lose the protection she needed from Kurt.

"Look, I'm sorry, really I am." She touched his arm and looked up at him as earnestly as she could. "I'm just nervous and, frankly, scared at being caught. I can't go to jail—not in the US and definitely not in Mexico. I get a little… bitchy when I'm on edge. Kurt, I know what you've sacrificed for me, and I do appreciate it, believe me, I do. I'll be a lot easier to get along with when we get our place near Mazatlán. I think I've found a little town, far enough away, yet close enough to civilization where we can live comfortably for the rest of our lives. Just you and me. Please, I really need you to help me get through this."

Kurt looked down at the wide pleading blue eyes. *You know she's working you. Get a backbone, man.*

The soft luscious lips were working their way into a small pout, and Ashlee's hand gripped his arm gently.

*Well, I need her as well. Let's play this out to the end.* "All right, Ashlee, I'll go along until we get our place, then we talk and set some rules."

He put his hand on hers, dropping it at the sight of the bartender heading their way.

"This is probation, understand?" he said.

"Understand." *He is so easy to work.* She almost smiled but squelched the urge.

Tony, the bartender, had walked around the bar to meet with the two police officers.

"Now, let me do the talking. Down here, folks get a little nervous around uniforms. I'll take the photo," he held his hand out, "and ask if they recognize this person. Will that help?"

Kurt pulled the wanted poster out and handed it to the young man. "More than you know. Thanks."

The trio headed out of the bar and moved down the promenade into each of the shops. Tony showed every airport worker the picture, asking if they'd seen this person. As Kurt and Ashlee had expected, no one recognized the picture of Elaine Madison. They were almost back to the bar when the public address system announced the boarding of their flight. They thanked the young bartender, tipped him an extra twenty dollars, and Ashlee promised she would stop and see him on her way back through. Kurt stood by stoically, keeping his temper and objections under control. As Kurt and Ashlee moved toward their boarding gate, he stopped. Ashlee bumped into the back of him. She started to complain.

"Can it, Ashlee. Follow me and don't ask questions."

The steel in Kurt's voice stopped her from the usual diatribe of complaints. She allowed him to take her hand and steer her into a phone alcove. He placed her in front of him and picked up the phone as if to call someone.

"What's going on?" she whispered.

"I swear I saw Corey Williams. Maybe I'm just being paranoid but I'd rather be safe than sorry." Kurt peered over his shoulder. He snapped his head around.

"Don't move. It's Corey, and he's walking past. I think he may have seen us. Just don't move."

Ashlee held her breath and followed Kurt's instructions. Minutes dragged by before he hoarsely whispered, "Let's get the hell out of here and on the plane."

The two peered into the concourse and, not seeing the Detective from Oakdale anywhere near, quickly walked to the boarding area. They showed their airline tickets stubs and flashed their badges and were immediately escorted to their seats on the plane.

"Damn, that was close." Ashlee grabbed for a cigarette.

Kurt took it from her, pointing to the no smoking sign. "Too close. I won't feel safe until this plane moves away from the terminal and gets in the air."

"On that, we both agree," Ashlee nodded.

## Sixteen

Corey and Riona waited fifteen minutes until the flight to Cancun with service extending to Mazatlán was announced. They boarded the plane and took their tourist class seats. Riona deferred to the middle seat, letting Corey sit next to the window. He furtively glanced out, tapping nervously on the armrests.

"Can you please stop that?" Riona asked.

"Stop what?"

"This is the first time you've flown, isn't it?" She watched his gaze scan the wings.

"Well, actually, yes. So what?" He cleared his throat.

Riona smothered a smile. "You probably have more chance of dying in that contraption you call a truck than you do on an airplane. Relax. Do you want to change places?"

"No, no thanks. I'll be fine. What's that?" Corey straightened in his seat clutching the arms of the seat.

"We're just being pushed backwards so the plane can move to the runway for takeoff."

The airliner taxied to its position in the waiting line. Half an hour passed before the engines revved up for departure. Riona watched Corey grip the armrests so tightly his knuckles appeared white. His face drained of color and he closed his eyes and licked his lips. The moment the plane lifted from the runway, he sucked in air and scrunched his eyes tightly. Within fifteen minutes, he heard the bell of a microwave oven. He opened one eye and looked around to face a smirking Riona.

"Did I hear a microwave oven in here?" he said incredulously.

"No. The buckle seat belt sign turned off. I guess it does sound like a microwave oven. You look green—must say, it's not your best color," she said. "You gonna be okay? If you want, we can change places in case you need to get sick."

"Thanks, but I think I'll be okay. I might even look out the window for a while," he said.

Riona raised her eyebrows.

"I said might," he answered.

"Good. I need sleep if we're gonna be running all over Mexico looking for Ashlee," Riona said.

She moved the seatback into the farthest reclining position and before Corey could respond had closed her eyes.

He watched the even, up and down motion of her chest. The red hair framed her face in wisps and her auburn lashes formed half-moons on her cheeks. He realized she had a sprinkling of light freckles across her nose and had to restrain himself from running his finger over them. *What are you dreaming of beautiful lady?*

~ * ~

Captain Martichev found himself watching the Irish reporter with interest. He had tried to stop her from coming with his unit on dangerous missions, but his men had begun to ask questions he didn't want to answer. The third week of September found him in a ditch next to this Ron Byrne person.

"Well, this is not how I envisioned spending the first week of fall."

He rose slowly to look over the rim of the ditch. A bullet whizzed past his combat helmet, zinging off the rock wall next to them. The road wound past their position and into town, but a roving band of Mujahadeen looking to kill Russians had pinned them down.

"Get the hell down," Riona yelled at the captain. "If you get yourself killed, Captain, how the hell will I get back to town?"

Riona's Russian language skills had drastically improved since she'd been keeping company with the Russian soldiers.

Captain Martichev slid down the lip of the ditch and leaned against the dirt wall. He shoved his helmet back and his steel gray eyes stared directly at Riona.

"Tell me, Irish, when were you going to tell me you're a woman?"

Riona sucked in the dust-laden air. "How—how did you find out?" she spat out.

"I doubted my own sanity the first night we met and you kissed me. I responded to the kiss of a man! That shook me hard, until a couple weeks later I watched you light one of your cigarettes. Something about the way you held the cigarette reminded me of my sister in Moscow then it dawned on me. The reason it reminded me of Natalya was that you're a woman, not the man you portray. All the feelings I'd been suppressing exploded. I've lost my perspective when it comes to you. This situation is a good example of why I can't have you in the field with me. I lose concentration of the problems at hand. I worry continuously about your safety, maybe more so than I would with a man or any of my soldiers. You need to leave, or I'll request a transfer for the sake of both our safety."

Martichev was shaking. He leaned toward Riona and, placing his hand behind her neck, pulled her to him. His mouth crushed hers. Backing off, his tongue searched for an opening into her soft warm sanctuary. She complied, moaning softly as their tongues met and intertwined. She welcomed his wandering hand on her breast and had begun to lose herself in his touch when a bullet hissed past their heads.

"Mmmm. This will have to wait until later," André murmured. He turned himself over and crawled to the top of the ditch. Carefully laying his rifle on the lip of dirt, he peered through the scope. A brief flicker of light up the road caught his attention. He maneuvered the Russian carbine in the direction of the flicker, held his breath, and pulled the trigger. A muffled scream followed the puff of dust he sighted in his scope. Allowing himself to slide down, he glanced at his watch.

"Let's give it ten minutes then crawl out of this dust pit. I think we'll be able to get back on the road to town."

Time moved with the speed of the Afghan camels. André nodded to Riona, but put his hand on her arm before she could move.

"By the way, what is your true name?"

She smiled. "Riona. The guys in the press room called me Ron for years."

"Well, Riona, follow me."

The captain poked his head above the berm. There was no sound, no guns firing; the road was empty of all traffic. He rose to his full height daring anyone to stop his movement. When no shots ricocheted past him, he pulled Riona up and they quick stepped into town. He escorted her to the hotel, stopping at the front desk to demand they prepare a hot bath for the reporter. Unnoticed by Riona, he slipped the desk clerk a week's worth of wages.

Riona turned around to thank the captain at the door to her room, but found an empty hallway. He had disappeared. She stumbled into her room, legs wobbly from squatting for so long. A knock on the door stopped her journey to her sink. She turned back to the door, hoping the captain had forgotten something. Her smile faded as she opened the door and saw the desk clerk facing her.

"Please, Mr. Byrne. The Captain has ordered a bath for you." He moved out of the way and two teenage boys dragged an old bathtub from years past inside her room, followed by several more young men holding steaming buckets of water. They placed the tub in the middle of her room and proceeded to pour the steaming water into the tub. When the tub was full, they left the room smirking and chattering in Dari.

Riona thanked the desk clerk, locking the door behind him. She would have argued, but every bone in her body ached and she hadn't had a decent bath in two weeks. She knew the down side of working in the frontier areas of small countries not familiar with industrial conveniences, but that's where news happened. And Riona was, first and foremost, a reporter determined to get the best story she could. She unbuttoned and unzipped her clothing, allowing it to drop where she stood. Once shed of her clothes, she stepped into the steaming bathwater. It was still warm in the daytime but when evening rolled around the temperatures dropped quickly to near freezing. Her skin reddened quickly but Riona refused to move until the water cooled to tepid. She quickly soaped and rinsed using a towel she had brought with her to dry off. A change of clothing, and she felt refreshed and awakened. She grabbed the clothing she had been wearing and proceeded to wash out the majority of the dust and dirt; no sense in letting good wash water go to waste.

She was hanging her clothes to dry when there was a knock on her door. *Damn, it's as busy as Piccadilly Square tonight.* She cautiously opened the door to a grinning Russian captain holding a bottle of vodka.

"Good evening, Riona. May I come in? I come bearing gifts." He smiled shyly.

Riona laughed. He looked so earnest she couldn't help herself. It appeared as though he too had taken a bath and, sniffing slightly, Riona realized he had shaved and somehow had located some aftershave lotion. He smelled of spices and vanilla. She opened the door and motioned him to come inside.

Her room was plain of design with no pictures on the walls, the only decoration being bullet holes sprinkled randomly over the wall surface, and no rugs on the floor. An old-fashioned wrought iron bedstead was the only ornamentation in the room she called home. She had one window that opened onto a small balcony, but it had been nailed shut due to the fighting. A simple stool served as her nightstand, with her traveling alarm clock, a hairbrush and her toothbrush resting on its rough-hewn top. In one corner, a table and two chairs stood up against the wall.

"Please have a seat at the table," she said.

She turned to find André within inches of her face. She wished she had remembered to bring some perfume.

"I have waited these two hours to be able to do this." André moved to her. He found her lips and gently introduced himself to her once again.

Riona melted into the door she leaned against, her defenses disappearing. She wanted this tall blonde Russian to sweep her off her feet and make love to her all night. *Where did that come from?* She tried her best to fight the urge she was feeling, but gave up. War had taught her life was too short, and love too brief to object.

André pulled back, smiling so broadly Riona noticed his dimpled cheeks for the first time since she had met him. *I'm lost.*

"Let us have some vodka and talk man to woman. There are many things I wish to know about you. Come." He grabbed her free hand and led her to the small table. He set the bottle on the tabletop and pulled out a chair for her to sit upon.

"Do you have something that can act as a cup?" he asked.

"No," she said.

"Then, we drink from the bottle." He opened the lid and took a swig. Once he finished he offered the bottle to Riona. She snatched the container from his hand and followed his lead. They sat and drank for the better part of an hour, talking and sharing their lives in the *other* world.

Riona looked into the steel gray eyes of the captain. "You haven't told me your proper name. What is it?"

The blonde Captain smiled. "André."

"André… André. I like it."

"That's good," he laughed.

"Well, André, I have a favor to ask of you," she said.

"Yes?"

"Make love to me all night."

The captain stopped and looked at the reporter. Even in the poor light of the hotel, this woman made him think of frescos in the palaces of Mother Russia. Her short red hair had grown out enough to encircle her face like a rosy halo, and the rich brown eyes made his heart pound each time he looked into them.

"I'm sorry. I've offended you." Riona blushed and started to get up from the table.

André gently grasped Riona's hand. "Oh, no. Please, Riona, you haven't offended me, you've honored me in a way I thought not possible. Allow me to try and please you as long as you desire." He pulled her to him, kissing her nose then tilting her chin so he could kiss her lips. He swept her into his arms, moved to the bed, and placed her gently on top of the covers. Walking to the middle of the room, he pulled the string that served as the on-off switch for the overhead bare bulb.

Riona felt the bed sink beneath his weight and his hand caress her cheek.

"Are you sure of this?" he asked.

"Yes."

They made love all night and into the daylight hours. With great regret, André left her in the morning, vowing to come to her the next night.

Riona found another unit to follow into battle so she wouldn't endanger herself and André. It hadn't been hard to do as the Russians craved the press coverage. She and André continued to meet in the evenings and stay together for long hours.

It had been three months since their first night together and, once again, they shared the warmth of a bed. Winter had swooped down upon Afghanistan and covered the barren landscape with snow, momentarily hiding the devastation of war. There was the coded knock upon the door and Riona bounded to open it for her lover.

André slid covertly into the room, quickly igniting the candle that had become their mode of light. Riona raised her eyebrows in question and started to speak. He motioned her to silence with the raising of his finger to his lips. He moved to the door and leaned his ear against the wooden wall. After a few moments, he moved to the bed and, patting the spot beside him, motioned for Riona to join him.

"I have finally received a package from home with something I asked my mother to send me." He pulled a small box from his great coat and, gently holding Riona's hand, turned her palm up and placed the box in her hand.

She looked up at him through her auburn lashes.

"André, what is this?"

"Please, open it for me."

She sucked in a deep breath and, lifting the top of the small white box, peered into it. Sitting on yellowing cotton batting rested a gold filigree ring with a large ruby surrounded by small diamonds. Riona gently pulled the ring from the box.

"This is absolutely gorgeous. Whose is it? Where did you get it? My God, André, is it real?"

"It is real, my love, and a family heirloom passed from mother to son." He slid from the bed to one knee and held Riona's other hand.

"Please agree to be my wife. I don't think I could live the rest of my life without you. Riona, please?" he asked.

"Oh—my—God, André." Riona looked down into the softened gray eyes. He was everything she wanted in a man, and they could make such beautiful children together.

"Yes, yes, I will marry you." She beamed.

He took the ring from her hand and placed it on her finger before he stood and pulled her to him. His kiss was hot and hungry, and they tumbled on the bed to make love until the new day. Morning dawned on the two lovers entwined in each other's arms. When the alarm went off, André swore in Russian and sat up in bed to turn it off but Riona had beaten him to it and silenced the offending clock.

"Good morning, my soon-to-be wife." André feathered kisses on her forehead and each eyelid.

"Hmmm, good morning, my soon-to-be husband." She reached for him and they melted together, making love before rising out of bed.

"I have something I must tell you," Riona started.

"As I have news for you," André replied.

"You go first," she said.

"I am being deployed further north for about a week, then I will return. Once this deployment is over, I will be shipped back to Russia. We will be able to get married before the thawed snow fills the Volga, my love. What is it you wish to tell me?" André turned on his side resting his head on his hand as he watched Riona.

"Deployed? North? André it's dangerous up north. Please be careful. Isn't there any way you can get assigned to Europe or the US?" she asked.

"I'm afraid not, my love. I am a soldier, not a diplomat. Do you not want to spend your life with me?"

Riona looked into the eyes of her lover and saw the hurt. "Of course I want to spend my life with you. I love you. We can discuss this further when you come back. Unfortunately, right now, we both have to work."

"Is that all you wanted to tell me?"

"Just that I love you."

"And I love you."

The couple shared what coffee Riona had saved and bid each other farewell. She was off to report on the rebuilding efforts of the farmers in the south, and he to fight in the north. They set a time to meet when he returned and, after a long, lingering kiss, said their goodbyes.

When Riona returned two days later, she noted the desk clerk looked at her with sad eyes and the hotel employees steered clear of her. She reached her room and opened the door, letting her bag drop to the floor. There was a note on her small table. It was written in Russian but she recognized the sergeant's name. He had attempted to write it in English for her benefit but had scratched through the effort.

She grabbed her pack containing her valuables and ran to the hut the Russian unit was utilizing as their quarters. She burst into the door. The subdued voices and drawn faces held a message she didn't want to hear. She looked at the sergeant and started shaking her head.

"No, please don't tell me he's gone. No," she heard herself say.

"I am sorry, but they were ambushed on their way home. No one survived." The sergeant looked to the ground and shook his head.

"NO!" Riona screamed and ran outside. She looked up and down the street and realized she had nowhere to run, so she walked back to the hotel, ignoring the snow and cold seeping through her boots. She lay on the bed and sobbed until her throat was raw and she had no tears. She fingered the ring she wore. It would serve no purpose for her to keep it. She searched for the little box it had come in and, when she'd located it under the bed, she placed the ring back inside. Her finger felt something hard under the cotton batting. Lifting the yellowed batting, she found a small envelope. She took the envelope out and turned it over. Her name had been written on the front in André's hand. She opened the lip with shaking fingers and turned it over. Out slid a silver necklace with a single unicorn hanging from the chain. The eye was a tiny green emerald peering at her. Inside was a folded piece of paper. Riona pulled it out and opened it.

"This necklace is like you, my love—rare and vanishing. Please wear it and think of me."

André had signed it, "Your husband."

Riona crumpled to the floor and began to sob. She would wear the necklace until she died, but her conscience wouldn't allow her to keep the ring. It was, after all, a family heirloom. She would return to the Russian unit Andre had commanded and ask the sergeant to personally deliver the ring back to Andre's family.

She already had a reminder of André she would carry home with her.

~ * ~

Corey watched his traveling companion in the seat next to him. Her dark auburn lashes fluttered against her cheek and she was moving in her seat, moaning low and mournfully. She kept reaching up and stroking the unicorn necklace.

He'd discovered the hard way, two black eyes early in his marriage before he'd learned to duck, to gently awaken someone from a bad dream. He gingerly laid his hand on Riona's arm. A chill spread over his body, causing the hair on the back of his neck to stand. He shook his head and reached for the overhead controls. He found the air in the off position. Riona moaned and he touched her arm again.

She relaxed at his touch. Her moaning stopped and the crease in her forehead eased. She sighed and tried to roll in his direction. He waited a moment, to let her continue sleeping. She stirred and slowly opened her eyes.

The flight attendant had been traveling down the aisle with the drink cart and reached their row.

"Would you like something to drink?" She asked pleasantly.

"Yes, I'd like an orange juice," Riona answered in perfect Russian.

The attendant looked at Corey and shrugged her shoulders.

"I speak Spanish but not what she's speaking, help."

Corey looked Riona square in the eye. "Do you realize you just asked the flight attendant for something speaking, what sounds like, Russian?"

Riona blushed crimson, her hand moving to the unicorn guarding her throat. She looked to the attendant and repeated in English, "I'm sorry. Could I get an orange juice?"

Smiling as if nothing had occurred, the attendant filled a glass with ice and handed the glass and a small bottle of orange juice to Riona. She raised her eyebrows in question at Corey who shrugged his shoulders.

Riona poured her drink and glanced sideways at Corey. He was watching her, but not asking the questions that had arisen in his mind.

"What?" she said.

"Nothing, I figure if you want me to know you'll tell me. I will say this, your Russian sounds pretty authentic. Oh, yeah, you were thrashing and moaning in your sleep quite a bit. Hope you caught whoever you were chasing." He turned and looked out the window at the ocean moving below the plane.

Riona drained the glass and set it on the tray she'd pulled down in front of her. She ran her finger around the top of the plastic glass while she considered whether or not to tell Corey about André.

After all, this was the man who'd had her motorcycle towed the first time they met. But then again, he'd jumped to her rescue when she'd foolishly passed out at the restaurant. Sitting in silence trying to decide if she should confide in him, a finger of icy cold moved down her back. Riona shivered and reached up to adjust the direction of the air conditioning spout only to find it closed. The column of cold wrapped around her, and she shivered again.

"You alright?" Corey's brow furrowed in concern.

"Yeah, just tired. Uh, did I mention any names while I was sleeping?" she asked.

"What's it worth to you for me to tell you?" Corey was grinning.

"Nothing, I just wondered." Riona crossed her arms.

"Actually, you were muttering in Russian…"

"Yes, Russian."

"…most of the time, so I wasn't able to understand it. There did seem to be something resembling a name, an André?"

"I see. Well, it's like this..." Riona's eyes twinkled wickedly as she continued in Russian: "...I went to Afghanistan, met a Russian Captain, fell in love, got engaged and lost him when he was killed. When I came back to the United States I requested to be assigned to all the hot spots of the world, trying to forget him, and finally settled in Billington about three years ago."

Corey's mouth was a straight line and his eyes had narrowed. "Very funny. Now why don't you tell me in English, so I can understand?"

"I don't think I'm ready to share. When the time is right, maybe. What about you? You speak any foreign languages? Got any kids? A wife? I don't know a thing about you. Have you always been a cop?"

Corey squirmed uncomfortably in his seat. *If I want to know her, I'd better come across with some info on myself.*

"I speak only tourist Spanish, you know; *cerveza, tequíla*, and *Dondé está el baño?* As far as kids, I've got five great kids, only I haven't seen them in about four years because my ex-wife moved them away in the middle of the night. She decided she needed to realize her potential, and Virginia wasn't karmic enough. I have no idea where they relocated and have been unable to find any clues, even with all the connections I have. I have no love life; therefore, I have no girlfriends. I work, go home, have a beer or two, watch TV and go to bed. I lead a very boring life and, yes, I've always been a cop. I got lucky. When I got out of high school, I took the community college law enforcement courses and, after passing the city exam, was hired to the Oakdale police force as a patrolman."

Riona eyed the man sitting next to her. His hazel eyes, more brown today, searched her face. He'd taken a chance and opened up to her. She could see by his pained eyes the part about his ex-wife and children had been difficult for him to tell her. *I don't believe it. He's got a crush on me.*

"Okay. I'll share a little with you, but that doesn't mean we're lifelong buddies."

Corey nodded.

"I speak several languages fluently; Russian, Spanish, French, Italian, German and Mandarin Chinese. I learn quickly, which came in handy when I was assigned all over the world to cover stories for a well-known news magazine. I'm an expert shot, have a black belt in Karate and can't carry a tune in a bucket, but can out-whistle anyone. I've never been married, and probably won't get married, because I'm not good at being in one place very long."

Her eyes dared him to say something but Corey kept his silence.

"What, no wisecracks?"

"After learning you have a black belt in Karate? My mama didn't raise no fool. No wisecracks." Corey grinned at her.

The plane began to shake and the humming sound of the flaps lowering silenced the exchange. Corey tightened his seatbelt and clutched the armrests. He looked out at the wing then scrunched his eyes shut. *That was a dumb thing to do.* The bile began to rise in his throat. He swallowed and began taking deep breaths.

"You're not gonna hurl on me are you? That's what those little brown bags are for," Riona smirked.

"Thanks for your concern. I hadn't thought about getting sick until you mentioned it." Corey opened one eye and glared at Riona.

She smiled sweetly at him. He shut his eyes tightly.

The plane bumped down on the runway. The screeching of the brakes made Corey grab the armrests tighter. The aircraft slowed and began to taxi to the terminal. He opened one eye and slowly opened the second. Peering out the window he saw the clear blue sky and greenery of the landscape. In the distance, the ocean glittered turquoise. A small strip of blinding white sand called an invitation.

"I wish we had time to stay. That ocean looks inviting." He sighed wistfully.

The passengers were moving about the cabin retrieving their carry-on bags from overhead and jostling for position. Once the plane docked, the flight attendant opened the hatch and the crush of humanity flowed out of the silver bird, chattering excitedly.

Corey and Riona waited until all the passengers had left. They unbuckled their seat belts and followed the crowd to the terminal. A quick check with the departure monitors showed their connecting flight wasn't set to leave for at least an hour. They found their way to a map of the airport.

"I've got to smell real air before we're captive for another four hours. I'm going out here." Corey pointed to an area marked as a sitting area. "You coming?"

"I could stand to get in the sun for a little while." Riona nodded and followed his lead.

~ * ~

Corey and Riona moved toward the exit indicated on the airport map. Each step they took brought the smell of spices, meat cooking and other food. Corey's stomach grumbled loudly. He looked down. "Hush. You're not hungry. You just think you are."

Riona laughed. "Maybe we should stop and eat?"

"No, I want to wait until we reach our destination, then I'll eat."

"It's up to you."

They continued through the walkway until they had reached their desired exit. Corey opened the door and followed Riona through to the peaceful courtyard. A whisper of breeze ruffled his hair and the hint of sea salt tickled his nose. There was also a teasing sweetness to the breeze. *Must be a local flower.*

Corey closed his eyes momentarily and let himself drift away.

"Hello?" Riona turned to glance at him.

Corey took a deep breath and started coughing. The once sweet air reeked of jet fuel. The thundering of a departing airliner emphasized this point.

"You ready to go inside yet? I'm roasting. It's hotter than the devil out here." Riona turned on her heel and went into the air-conditioned terminal.

Corey looked at the peaceful courtyard and sighed. *Just two minutes of peaceful quiet to let my eardrums recuperate. Oh, well.* He followed Riona inside the terminal. They stood uncertainly for a moment until his stomach rumbled again.

"That's it. I can't take the sound of your stomach trying to tell you food is necessary. Come on. We're going to eat, and I'm buying. I knew the police department kept you on a tight budget but this is ridiculous. Let's find a McDonald's. Almost every country in the world has one."

Corey recalled passing a food court on their way to the courtyard and registering the trademark smell of McDonald's French fries. They started back past the shops with postcards and remembrances of Cancun, the check-in counters for other airlines, bathrooms, and cul-de-sac's of phones. As he passed the phone nook, the hair on the back of his neck began to raise, his skin forming goose bumps. Stopping in the middle of the concourse he turned completely around, slowly taking in the landscape.

Ahead of him, Riona walked confidently. Sensing the lack of his presence, she turned to see him standing in the middle of the walkway, visually searching for something. She walked back to him.

"What now?" she asked.

"Have you ever gotten the sensation someone is watching or following you?" Corey's face had lost all its color. The intense expression on his face warned her he was serious.

"Actually, I have. It's been happening a lot lately. What about this spot has you spooked?" Riona felt her shoulders tighten with tension and watched his eyes scan the area.

"Not spooked just… I feel like someone or something here is familiar." He turned to face her.

Riona noted an airport security guard talking with one of the shopkeepers. They seemed to be in a heated discussion. She realized his uniform was almost identical to the one Corey wore. She relaxed her shoulders and started to smile.

She pointed to the guard. "Maybe you caught him moving out of the corner of your eye and thought it might be Kurt and Ashlee. You've got to admit their uniforms look a lot like yours."

Corey turned and witnessed the guard and shopkeeper. Feeling the hair on the back of his neck rise slightly, he looked at Riona and shrugged. "I think you're right. Looks just like our uniform. Let's go eat. I'm starved."

The two picked up their pace to the fast food restaurant.

~ * ~

Corey bit into the double cheeseburger and closed his eyes in ecstasy. There really was nothing like the taste of an American cheeseburger and French-fries. Riona had set her tray on the table and was preparing to sit in the chair to eat.

The public address system announced something in Spanish but Corey was so wrapped up in his lunch he didn't hear it. He wouldn't have understood it anyway, so he dismissed the sound.

"Damn it!" Riona jumped from her seat and bolted onto the walkway, sprinting back toward the gate where they had disembarked. She returned five minutes later scowling and swearing in Russian.

By that time, Corey had finished his lunch and was sipping his cola.

"Dare I ask what the problem might be?"

"Did you hear the announcement over the PA?" She glared at her food.

"Yeah, but since I don't speak Spanish it just sounded like gibberish to me." He slurped the last of his soda through the straw.

"Well, that gibberish, as you put it, was an announcement for a flight to Mazatlán. One I had no idea existed. If we could have gotten on that plane we'd save ourselves the one hour layover we're currently experiencing." She plopped into the chair and lifted the top of her burger. "Not really hungry now." She moved the food to the center of the table.

Corey fixed his eyes on the uneaten burger, his stomach growling loudly.

She pushed the cold burger and fries in his direction. "*Bon appetít*."

Finishing the burger and fries, he sat back in the orange plastic chair.

"Boy, I could sure use a nap. What say we go back to that little courtyard?" He looked at the frowning Riona.

"Yeah, why not, nothing better to do." She rose from her chair and headed out to the concourse walkway.

The twosome stopped at a newsstand where Riona bought a Mexican soap opera digest, a newspaper from Mazatlán, and the Mexican version of the international magazine where she'd been a reporter. They continued their stroll until they arrived at the empty courtyard, where Corey found a bench that would support him. He lay down to sleep. Riona opted for a seat in the shade. She'd been reading for a few moments when she realized Corey was fast asleep. However, unlike any other man of size, he wasn't snoring. She got up and went over to him. The creases in his forehead had disappeared. His eyes were less lined at the corners and his whole face was placidly peaceful. She realized he looked ten years younger than she could recall. In fact, he was quite handsome. His red-brown hair was beginning to turn silver at his temples, giving him a rather distinguished look.

She remembered how dark his eyes had become whenever he talked about Ashlee Anderson. The man was fiercely loyal to his friends, and Ashlee had tried to hurt a very good friend of his. Watching Corey talk about how Ashlee had hurt Justin, his friend, Riona decided she didn't want to be on the receiving end of his anger. She reached out and smoothed away a stray lock of hair from his forehead. *Oh, man. I'd better be careful or I'll fall for this guy.*

She jerked her hand away just as he moved and sighed. She backed away and finished reading her magazines. This man was beginning to grow on her and she was feeling a little panicked. *Some space and perspective will cure any emotions I might start feeling. This is business, this is business, this is business.*

Twenty minutes later, Corey awoke and sat up. He stretched his arms and leaned over to unfold his back. Once he'd straightened all the kinks in his muscles, he stood.

"Shall we start toward the loading gate? I think we can make it with about five minutes to spare." He smiled at Riona.

She felt her heart melt at a dimple in his right cheek she hadn't seen before. His relaxed face and attitude was making her view him differently. *He's really kind of sexy. Stop it!*

"Sure, let's get going." She closed her newspaper and gathered everything up, tucking it under her arm.

The two set a fast pace to the loading gate, arriving in time to check in and go directly to their seats on the plane.

"Next stop Mazatlán," Corey said.

## Seventeen

Corey cinched his seatbelt tightly and gripped the arms of the seat until his knuckles were white, as the plane engines revved up for takeoff.

"Still can't get the hang of this?" Riona smirked.

"No. I don't know how you can possibly sleep with all this noise and the thought we could plunge to our death at any moment," Corey spoke through clenched teeth.

"Years of practice. When I was an international reporter, I learned to grab any sleep I could. When you drop behind the lines of a war, any war, you have to keep your eyes open to stay alive, so you take every opportunity to sleep. When you're flying, you're a captive audience. Not much to do and lots of time not to do it in, so, I sleep. I'll be ready to go once we hit the ground in Mazatlán. You might try it yourself." Riona waited until the plane had leveled off at cruising altitude before she dropped the seat into the reclining position. Within minutes, she was breathing slowly and evenly.

Corey looked at her angelic face and resisted the urge to touch her cheek.

*Black belt in karate, black belt in karate; remember she could make you a soprano with very little effort. I might as well try to get some rest. Riona's right. It may be some time before we get a chance to relax again. Okay, here goes.*

He leaned his seat back, loosening the seatbelt so he could breathe. Closing his eyes, he allowed himself to drift into the netherworld of twilight sleep.

~ * ~

Riona cursed. She'd missed her period and figured it was the stress of losing André, but when she'd started throwing up first thing in the morning and waking up in the middle of the night to visit the bathroom, she knew she was in trouble. *This is all I need now.*

Raised a Catholic, she knew she wasn't going to terminate the life now living within her. *What the hell am I gonna do with a kid? Maybe the sergeant knows if André had family who would take care of this child... that's the best solution. I'll ask him.*

She grabbed her coat off the bed and bounded down the stairs, quickly walking the several blocks to the company headquarters. The sergeant sat at the table frowning down at the papers strewn across the top.

"Good morning, Ron." He looked up as Riona entered; the breeze from outside ruffling the papers under his hand.

"Morning, Sarge. I need to ask you about Captain Martichev, personal information that is very important to me right now." She plopped down in the wooden chair across from him.

"What do you need?" Sarge tapped the pen on the table.

"We need to talk in confidence, just you and me. Will that be possible here?" She waved her arm at the small room.

"Da."

"How long have you known I was a woman?" She looked directly into his eyes.

He laughed, and Riona caught the faint aroma of stale alcohol and cigarettes.

"Since the first time I saw you. Captain was too busy trying to deny his attraction to you because he thought you were a man, but I knew. You don't walk like a man. You don't eat like a man, and even though you are good at keeping up with us, you don't drink like a man. I've known for a long time. And now, you are with child, are you not?"

His hazel eyes twinkled as the corners of his mouth curved up slightly.

Riona threw her hands up in the air. "Why do I bother? Yes. I'm pregnant, but Sarge, I can't keep this child. Some people are meant to be mothers and some aren't. I'm in the second group. I might've thought about it when André was alive, but not now. That's where I need your help. Does he have any family in Russia willing to raise his child?"

The sergeant turned to a small filing cabinet behind him and opened the top drawer. He retrieved a brown file which he then opened on top of the papers cluttering his desk. Riona watched his lips move slightly as he read the information inside the folder.

"I remember him speaking about a former wife. They married out of secondary school when she convinced him she was pregnant. After a few months, she made a big fuss about losing the child. He'd always suspected it was a ruse so she could move out of her parents' home into her own place. When André went into the service, word reached him she was dating other men. He took leave and they got divorced. However, they kept in touch. Through the years, their relationship became friendship, and that's when he learned she'd been unable to have children. He'd commented, although he could've been bitter because she'd tried to fool him, he knew she'd have made a good mother. André's mother is too old to raise more children, and his sister, a ballerina, defected to the West ten years ago."

Shrugging his shoulders, he turned his hands toward the ceiling. "I'm truly sorry, but it is all I can offer."

Riona sat in the hard wooden chair weighing her options as the sergeant watched her.

"How do I make this happen?" she asked.

"Leave it to me. I will make the arrangements. Keep in touch." He stuck out his hand.

Riona grasped his hand in her own. André's line would continue, and the Russian heritage he was so proud of would not die with him.

~ * ~

Riona had contacted her editor, Russell Maddox. The gaunt, hatchet faced, man with thinning dishwater blonde hair and dull blue eyes had always been Riona's favorite opponent.

They'd literally argue over the time of day, and spent many evenings in verbal battle at their favorite watering hole, Clancy's Irish Pub. Folks often made the mistake of thinking they'd been married because of the volatile arguing, but soon found themselves vehemently corrected about the relationship.

Riona put in a call Tuesday afternoon, Afghani time.

"What do you want now?" Russ' reedy voice grumped to his caller.

"Nice to hear from you, too, Russ. I need you to transfer me to the Russian office as soon as you can."

"What the hell for? Isn't Afghanistan dangerous enough for you? You need to be an American in Russia?" he grouched.

Riona pictured him pacing back and forth in front of his desk, chewing the right side of his bushy handlebar mustache.

"I need to be in Russia to follow up on the unit you sent me to cover. They've received orders to deploy back to the motherland, and I'd like to report on how they adjust to civilian life after a year in this hellhole," she answered.

"Humph. Well, it would make sense to see if they have as much trouble as our boys did coming back from Vietnam. All right, but you gotta find your own way to Russia. Call me when you get there."

Riona smiled as the phone clicked in her ear. She needed to talk to the sergeant again.

~ * ~

The sergeant was putting files in a box on the top of the table that served as his desk.

"Ron! I didn't expect to see you so soon. What is it I can do for you?" He continued to put items into the box.

"Sarge. I need to find transportation to Moscow. The way I'm feeling right now, I won't be able to ride in the troop carrier for as long as it will take to get there. Do you have any options you can offer?" She pulled up the chair and sat.

"Let me see." He went to the radio and started working the switches and buttons. In a dialect Riona didn't recognize, he briefly spoke with someone and hung up. "I can secure you a helicopter ride to Mother Russia. I have an acquaintance who owes me a big favor. This evens our debt. You'll need to be ready in one hour. Be on the north road out of town, bags packed, and wear this helmet." He handed her André's combat helmet marked with his captain's insignia on the front. She raised her eyes at the sergeant.

"Do you want to go?"

Riona nodded yes.

"Then don't question what I tell you. Just do it, and act as though it should happen. No one will suspect you if you act like you have the authority. The pilot knows the story, but there's no need for anyone else to have the information. Captain Martichev..." the sergeant clicked his heels together and saluted Riona, "...I will look forward to seeing you in Moscow. You will buy me dinner, da?"

Riona affected her best salute.

"It will be my pleasure, Sergeant."

The two shook hands, and Riona went to pack her belongings. She was headed to Russia to finish her story.

# Eighteen

The young helicopter pilot resembled the stereotypes for the perfect Aryans that Hitler had touted during World War II. Tall, blonde, blue eyed and breathtakingly handsome, she found herself comparing him to André. He was polite as he ushered her into the helicopter and disappeared into the cockpit. When the bird lifted suddenly into the air, Riona fought to keep from throwing up—captains in the Russian Army didn't throw up, and she felt she was representing André.

Seven, bone-jarring, body shaking, nausea producing hours later, the helicopter set down on a landing pad near the Kremlin in Moscow. Not even a fuel stop near the middle of the journey had helped to settle Riona's stomach. She looked pleadingly at the handsome young pilot.

"Is there a bathroom nearby?" She began to feel the bile rising in her throat.

"Ma'am?"

Riona figured out later that her face must have been chartreuse, because the questioning look on the young pilot's face quickly changed to one of recognition. He quickly escorted her to the bathroom inside the hanger of the landing field where she unceremoniously dumped her morning meal. Swishing her mouth out, she realized she needed a nap more than anything else.

The young pilot appeared at her side dutifully sliding his arm under hers. She jerked her arm away.

"What are you doing?" She glared at him.

"Well, I—I thought…" He dropped his hand to his side.

"Tell me, young man, you've never been so hungover you spent the next day throwing up all day?"

She fisted her hands on her hips.

The young pilot grinned sheepishly and shook his head. "*Nyet*."

"Well, combine that with a seven hour helicopter ride from hell and you can guess how I feel." She turned and stomped toward the grounded chopper. "I'll be glad to get some decent vodka to drink. Maybe I won't be so sick next time."

The young pilot scurried to catch up to the tall reporter.

"Excuse me, ma'am? We've already taken your baggage to the international hotel downtown. You've been checked through to your room. If you'll follow me, I'll see to it you arrive safely. It's not recommended for a non-Muscovite to roam the streets unescorted these days."

The pilot pointed her in the direction of a black vehicle that reminded Riona of the taxis in London. It had seen better days, but was better than trying to figure out the local subway. At the moment she was desperately in need of a lie down. She walked to the vehicle and allowed the pilot to open her door.

He turned to a soldier standing nearby and shouted he was taking the captain to the hotel and would be back within the hour. The soldier nodded, and Riona and the pilot sped away into the streets of André's hometown.

One of Riona's first assignments had been to cover the reaction of the Russian students when it was first announced troops would be sent to Afghanistan. Time had not changed much in the few years she'd been away. The buildings, built after World War II, still dominated the skyline with their military repressiveness. She was certain she'd be able to get around once she was rested.

At the hotel, the young pilot assisted her from the vehicle and handed her the room key. He directed a sullen looking porter to escort her to her suite and, with a click of his highly polished black boots, bid her farewell. Riona thanked him for his assistance and watched the car slide into the traffic from the curb. Once the officer had left the porter melted into the interior of the hotel. She would've liked to study the façade but the overwhelming stench of exhaust was making her nauseous. She entered the hotel and walked to the ancient elevator along the sidewall. Smirking, she directed the aged operator to let her out on the sixth floor. After a shuddering journey upward, she was released onto the correct floor and found the room indicated on the key. Inside, she double locked the door and lay on the bed. Her stomach rolled and sent her fleeing to the private bathroom to empty its contents. *I'm not sure I'll live through this.*

She sighed, as she lay down and put a cool, damp washcloth on her forehead. Closing her eyes, she allowed sleep to overtake her.

~ * ~

The darkened room confused Riona. *Where the hell am I?*

She sat up slowly, allowing her eyes to adjust to the darkness. The curtains over the window showed the unmistakable signs of former wealth. Heavy velvet and bordered with gold, they flowed from the twenty-five foot ceiling to the floor. The furniture was heavy and dark, and the bed she lay upon was lumpy but the velvet spread showed gold threads throughout. The carpet upon the floor had been elegant and plush when first put down fifty years previously, but time had not been kind and currently its state was threadbare. She slowly pulled the musty air into her lungs and clutched her stomach.

*Oh, yeah, Moscow. Wonder when I'll hear from the sergeant.*

Riona rose from the bed and, crossing to the window, grasped the gold cord on the side of the curtains. She drew back the velvet coverings and glimpsed the sight of Moscow at night. Sucking in her breath sharply, she surveyed the view from her window. *Lord, I'd forgotten how beautiful this city is.*

A rumbling from her stomach reminded her she had dispelled her breakfast and not eaten since early in the morning. Picking up the ancient rotary phone, she dialed the operator and asked if the kitchen was still available for meals. A short list was recited and Riona decided to try soup and bread. Half an hour later, a knock on her door revealed a bored looking room service attendant holding a covered tray. She ushered him into the room and handed him five dollars. She watched the bored expression flicker for an instant then thc borcdom returned to his face. Ushering him out the door, she noted the spring of his step belying his expression. Once she finished the simple meal, she felt exhaustion overtake her again. She drew a bath, watching the steam from the water rise in white diaphanous clouds that fogged the mirror over the sink. Shedding clothes heavy with a week's worth of Afghani dirt, Riona dipped a toe into the steaming water. *Damn that's hot!* A grin spread across her face. *Real hot water.*

She slipped into the tub, an inch at a time. The war and hard dirt beds with bed bugs melted away with the dissolving grime. Using the last of her rose scented soap, she scrubbed as hard as she dared from the tip of her head to the bottom of her feet, feeling certain she had removed the top layer of her skin as well.

*I only wish I could wash away the sorrow I feel. André, I wanted to see Moscow again, but with you not just your memory.*

She sighed deeply as she drained the tub and toweled dry. Her energy spent in bathing, she crawled into bed and slept until the rays of the rising sun washed across her face the next morning.

Riona spent a leisurely week retracing her steps in Moscow. Coffee shops and restaurants she had haunted during her first visit years earlier hadn't changed much. The clientele seemed younger, but still spoke fervently of Mother Russia and how she needed change. This was done in muted tones so as not to attract attention of any of the *politburo* that might've wandered in for coffee.

On Wednesday, she met with the young man who was to be her photographer. They'd sat in the shop and drank Russian tea while setting up a deadline schedule. It had been difficult as the young photographer was a handsome single man and the college coeds were quite fascinated with him. They'd agreed on time deadlines, and he'd secured the numbers of several attractive young ladies before the afternoon ended.

On the Friday evening, Riona sat in her suite, finishing her report on the typewriter the magazine had sent over when she was interrupted by a knock on her door. She moved slowly—she had learned quick movement would send her to the bathroom in a flash—and when she opened the door, she found herself looking into the eyes of the sergeant.

"Sarge!" She embraced the soldier and ushered him into her suite. As she prepared to close the door, he stuck his hand out.

"I have brought a visitor for you to meet." His eyes twinkled wickedly and a smile began to form on his lips. He waved a small figure into the room then closed the door.

"Riona Byrne, this is Svetlana Martichev." The sergeant stepped aside to introduce a small boned, red haired, blue-eyed beauty who stood no taller than five foot one inch.

Riona looked down at the tiny figure. *At least you're consistent, André.*

The tiny Russian extended her slender white hand and said slowly in heavily accented English, "It is a pleasure to make your acquaintance, Ri-ri-oh-nah."

Riona hid the smile she felt trying to overtake her lips. *She'll be a perfect mother for Anton.*

She took the small hand into her own and in her well-used Russian answered, "The pleasure is mine, Mrs. Martichev. I hope we'll be able to come to a mutual agreement that'll benefit us all."

The tiny Russian gasped and stepped backward. "You speak Russian?"

"Yes. I was here previously working for my magazine. Speaking the language made interviewing people so much easier. There are some words that just don't have the same impact when spoken in English. So, when I got the assignment, I took Russian from our correspondent at the magazine. It has served me well."

Riona noticed the woman's agitation and suggested they go to the bar around the corner to continue their conversation. The sergeant nodded his affirmation, and the small woman was in the hall before Riona could retrieve her jacket from the back of the chair.

"She seems so nervous," she commented to the sergeant.

"KGB," he mouthed to her.

"Oh." She'd almost forgotten the dreaded secret police that kept tabs on the entire country.

The bar was three blocks and light years away from the journalist's hotel. People stood elbow to elbow gesturing animatedly while conversing. A cloud of blue haze hung heavy over the room and a jukebox blasted a mixture of popular Russian pop ballads and old American rock and roll, drowning conversation in the corner near it. The sergeant led the way to a table near the front window. He propped it open and set Riona near the opening. Gasoline and diesel fumes tainted the breeze, but were less toxic than the smoke laden air closer to the bar.

Riona and Svetlana made small talk while the sergeant got their drinks, pushing his way up and back from the bar. Setting the glasses in front of them, Riona raised her eyebrows at him when she realized he'd brought her plain tea.

"It is for your own good, and you know it," he replied gruffly.

Svetlana looked at Riona then the sergeant.

"You haven't told her yet, have you?" he questioned Riona.

She shook her head slowly and he raised his eyebrows. "Did you expect me to say something?"

"No, but I did want you to be here when I proceeded," she said.

Svetlana scowled and crossed her arms over her chest. "May I ask what is going on? If you two wish to be alone, why am I here?" She glowered at them.

Riona sighed deeply, took a sip from her tea and started her story. The brief history of her affair with the captain and her impending pregnancy quickly took the frown off the face of the tiny Russian woman sitting across from her.

"I was raised," Riona lowered her voice and leaned in toward her tablemates, "catholic, so I don't believe in terminating a pregnancy, but I can't raise a child by myself and wouldn't ask any child to live my lifestyle. I asked the sergeant, when I discovered my condition, if he knew of you and I asked what you were like. He had high praise for you."

Svetlana blushed. She leaned back in her chair. "What is it you want of me?"

Taking a sip of tea, Riona sat for a moment then looked directly into the sapphire eyes searching her face.

"Would you consider taking my child and raising him or her as your own?"

Svetlana sat on the edge of her chair slowly rotating the glass of vodka with her fingertips. She peered into the liquid, her face unreadable.

*Oh, God. I've insulted her. What the hell will I do if she says no? I can't raise this child by myself and Sarge says André's mother is too old.*

"Why me?" The sapphire eyes had turned slate gray.

"I understand when you discovered you were unable to have children you made some excuse to André about needing to find yourself, and you gave him a divorce. He once said it was the most selfless act he'd ever had anyone do for him."

"He knew?" The eyes widened in shock.

"Yes, he knew. When he spoke of you, it was with tenderness and caring. I was hoping you would raise his child in the culture he loved so much. Will you consider it?"

Riona held her breath as the woman in front of her contemplated a decision that would change both their lives.

"I will," Svetlana held up her finger, "but with one condition."

"What?" Riona furrowed her brow.

"You must come live with me now so that the child will have the taste for Russian food from the beginning."

"Are you serious?"

"Very."

"All right, but won't that put your family in danger?" Riona asked.

"I believe you might be able to pass for my country cousin. If you come to the house a week from Friday, around noon, we will be able to make this work. It will give me time to explain to my mother and take a trip out of the country. When I come back, I'll mimic the symptoms of early pregnancy. In eight months or so, I'll have an early delivery at home. No one need be the wiser, and you'll be able to move on with your own life. Have you thought of a name?" Svetlana's eyes were once again sapphire.

"For a son, I decided Anton Andreyovich would be fine. I had not considered a girl's name, so the decision is yours to make. I'll contact Sarge a week from Friday and we'll move forward with this plan. Anything else?" Riona asked.

"I hate to sound like a capitalist, but what about money? My mother and I share a small flat just outside Moscow and expenses are tight." Svetlana signaled the harried waiter for another drink.

"I'll work on some explanation for my editor and see to it that you and your mother are reimbursed with a large stipend for your generosity toward me. It will be in place before I come to your front door. Will that work?" Pushing the tea glass away, Riona settled back in her chair.

"That will do fine. I am of two minds about this. I hate that André cared for you, but it will give me the child of his I have always wanted. For that, I thank you." She turned and looked for the waiter. "It would be nice to have a drink before I'm one hundred."

Riona excused herself and, handing the Sarge a fifty dollar bill, thanked them both. A quick walk to the hotel and she was in her room. She changed out of her clothes and crawled into bed. Exhaustion crept into her bones and she allowed sleep to overtake her. Her last thoughts were of André.

*He'll have the child he wanted so desperately. I can sense Svetlana will be a good mother and will keep in touch with André's family.*

~ * ~

The move went smoothly. While Riona's editor complained about her moving in with a Russian family and having to pay as if she were in the hotel, she swore to him he would have a series of articles so incredible that the magazine would be nominated for a Pulitzer Prize. It was a bold move on her part, but proved prophetic.

Her reporting on Svetlana's *pregnancy*, as the left-behind wife of a war hero, pushed up the circulation of the magazine twofold. When Anton was born, the family received gifts from all over the world. Riona loved André's family and was accepted by Svetlana's, but never bonded with the woman who would mother her child. An agreement was made between them; Riona would be Anton's *aunt* and they would send updates as often as they could.

Two months after his birth, a thinner, sadder Riona requested, and received, a transfer to another hot spot of the world. She walked away from Russia with no regrets.

## Nineteen

The plane leveled out and the seat belt sign turned off. Kurt left a sleeping Ashlee to visit the bathroom. The close call with Corey had upset his system and his stomach was reacting. *Or maybe the bartender at the airport in Cancun was trying to be funny by giving me the local water.* By the time he returned to his seat, Ashlee had sat up and was reading a magazine.

"Where'd you get that?" he asked.

"If you hadn't been so busy gawking at the flight attendants, you would've noticed the cabin side wall of the kitchen area has holders with all kinds of magazines," Ashlee snapped.

"Jealous?" he smirked.

"In your dreams. We need to discuss what we're going to do when we get to Mazatlan." Ashlee tucked the magazine in the pocket of the seat in front of her.

"What's to discuss? We get off the plane, go pick up our weapons, flash Elaine's picture around, get a car, and find a place to stay. Is that too much for your little head to comprehend?" Kurt raised an eyebrow as he looked at Ashlee.

He knew he'd stepped over the bounds when she turned slowly and pinned him with an icy stare.

"No," she said through gritted teeth. "It's not *too much* for my head to wrap around. But I would think you, of all people, would know it's not going to be that easy. You don't just waltz into a foreign police station, check in and check out. We'll be split up and questioned, separately, about why we're here and how long we expect to be in the country. They'll run a check on the weapons. If, and only if, they buy our story, they'll let us go on our way. We'll be required to check in to every police department along the way and fly out on the date we said we would be leaving. Now, what part of that did my head not wrap around?"

Kurt mumbled something unintelligible.

"Whatever. We're here to find Elaine, aka Ashlee, because someone in the United States pointed us in this direction. They remember her vacationing here and commenting that if she ever had the chance she would move here in a heartbeat. Then, we'll take our weapons and, after picking up a rental car, head downtown to rent two, count them, two rooms. Can you remember that?"

"Yeah."

"Good. I'm going to try to get some rest. Why don't you do the same?" Ashlee pulled down the blackout shade and turned away from Kurt.

He fumed quietly. If he hadn't been forced to hand over the money he might have thought of putting her in her place, but he was going to have to use a credit card even his wife didn't know about. *Surely there has to be an upside to this. If things don't get better, I'll turn Ashlee in myself and plead temporary insanity.*

He felt fingers on his chin and his face was turned toward Ashlee. Her big blue eyes looked deeply into his and she pulled him to her. Her lips caressed his as she slid her hand around the back of his neck pulling him to her. At some point she'd lowered the armrest and wiggled herself against Kurt. He nestled his hand inside her clothing, cupping her breast. She broke long enough to moan quietly in his ear. "God, that feels good. Please don't stop."

She allowed him to explore her with his darting tongue. His thumb found her hardened nipple, and he slid his body closer. She pushed her breast to his hand while her mouth hungrily searched for more. Pulling back, she looked at him with glistening eyes.

"The movie has started. Why don't we go freshen up—together? If we work this right, no one will even notice."

Ashlee slunk out of the seat and strolled toward the bathroom. At the door, she turned to see if Kurt was following. He'd been behind her by only three steps. She opened the door and stepped inside. Three seconds later, there was a knock. Opening the metal access enough to see out through the wall mirror, Ashlee admitted Kurt to the small cubicle. He started to speak but she put her finger to his lips and shook her head negatively. Eyes glittering lustily, she put his hand inside her blouse and began to unzip his pants.

"Welcome to the Mile High Club," she whispered, licking her lips lasciviously.

Twenty minutes later, Ashlee demurely slipped out of the cubicle, closing the door behind her. Smiling smugly, she strolled to her seat and sat down. Kurt joined her after sufficient time had passed.

"That was incredible." He leaned his seat back.

"Yes, it was. Almost makes flying worthwhile." Ashlee smiled and plumped her pillow. *That'll keep you coming back for more, you weasel. I've got something planned for you that you'll remember for the rest of your life.*

~ * ~

The flight attendant gently shook Ashlee then Kurt.

"Folks, folks—we're close to landing, and we need you to bring your seat backs up and buckle your belts." She continued down the aisle, gently waking other passengers.

Kurt looked at Ashlee and grinned. "We're twenty-four hours from our new life."

"Yeah, twenty-four hours." Ashlee looked out the window at the mountains passing below. A plan had begun to formulate since the plane had departed Cancun. The necessity to keep Kurt around would end when they got their weapons through the police offices at the airport in Mazatlán. She had her money back in her own pocket, and an idea of where she wanted to disappear. A wait of three to six months and she would be able to bring her daughter from the United States to live with her. She was finally going to live her dream—reveling in the moon in Mazatlán. A smile turned the corners of Ashlee's mouth up.

"Something you want to share?" Kurt eyed the Cheshire cat type grin on Ashlee's face.

She leaned over and gently kissed him on the cheek. "Later."

The jet landed uneventfully, and the couple waited until most of the passengers had departed the plane. They took a flight attendant aside and asked her to contact the pilot who was holding their weapons. She picked up the intercom and spoke with the pilot. She nodded and turned to Kurt.

"He asked me to verify you are police officers. May I see your identification?"

Kurt and Ashlee pulled their wallets out, handing them to the attendant. She took the individual pieces of identification out and turned them over running a fingernail along the edges.

Kurt threw a sidelong glance at Ashlee who casually stood against the wall of the galley.

Deciding the ID's were authentic, the attendant confirmed to the pilot everything appeared to be in order. The door of the cockpit opened and the black box containing their weapons was handed out. Kurt grabbed the box and thanked the pilot and attendant. He motioned for Ashlee to lead them through the jet way. The two strode briskly to the central building and found the security office. Kurt moved to the chest-high desk that divided the room. Ashlee sat in the wooden chair against the wall.

Kurt asked the only person visible in the office, "Do you speak English?"

The uniformed man behind a government-issue desk looked him up and down.

"A little. What can I do for you?"

"I need to speak with your supervisor, please."

"What is this about? Maybe I can help."

Kurt reached for his wallet and displayed his identification. "I'm a police officer from America looking for a suspect I believe has fled to your city. I want to be able to bring my weapons with me and carry them as I hunt for her."

The clerk behind the desk blinked several times and frowned slightly.

"I'm sorry, but I'll have to get someone else to help you. I don't understand."

Kurt's shoulders slumped and he turned to Ashlee.

"I hope I don't have to go through this a hundred times. I'd like to relax and have a beer."

Ashlee sighed and rolled her eyes at him. She stood and walked to the desk divider but as the clerk opened his mouth to speak, Ashlee interrupted him and spoke in Spanish.

"Excuse me, senor, but do you have a *Federalé* stationed in this office?"

The clerk nodded and picked up the phone, speaking in rapid Spanish.

"Officer Mendoza? There is an American policewoman out here wishing to speak to you. Yes, sir. Thank you."

He turned to Ashlee. "Please have a seat. He'll be with you in a moment."

The two American officers sat down in the simple wooden chairs to wait. Kurt turned to Ashlee.

"Why didn't you tell me you spoke Spanish?" he groused.

"You didn't ask." Ashlee closed her eyes and leaned her head against the wall.

A door in the back opened and a tall caramel skinned man in a *Federal* uniform emerged. Black wavy hair glistened as he walked under the fluorescent lighting, and his dark eyes took in the two American officers sitting against the wall. With long, easy strides, he crossed the office in a few steps. He stood at the desk divider, a blinding white smile creasing his tanned face. "*Habla español?*" he asked.

Kurt and Ashlee stood up and crossed to the divider.

"*Hablo y comprendo pero el.*" She nodded her head toward Kurt. "*No habla.*"

"Well, then, so we understand one another, I'll speak English. I'm Lieutenant Mendoza of the Federal Mexican Police. You are?" He proffered a handshake.

"I—uh—I'm Officer Kurt Lee, and this is Officer Elaine Madison."

Kurt extended his hand to meet the Mexican official's firm handshake. The man extended his hand toward Ashlee. Kurt watched the lieutenant's eyes rake over Ashlee, as she licked her lips lasciviously. He felt as though he was interrupting a private moment. He shook off the feeling.

"How may I serve two of America's finest?" The lieutenant's English was unimpeded with any accent.

Kurt reiterated the tale of being on the trail of Ashlee Anderson to the officer, and wanting to carry his weapon with him. The Mexican officer nodded his head.

"Well, Officer Lee, if you'll follow me, we can get this on tape and check out your references. Please leave your weapons with the desk sergeant. It shouldn't take long." Mendoza motioned for Kurt to come behind the barrier and follow him.

"Uh, is it really necessary? Shouldn't Officer Madison come with me?" Kurt chewed his lower lip.

"Actually, Officer Lee, since the terrorist attack on America we have increased our own security measures, and this will take but a moment. I'll question and record Officer Madison's statement as soon as you and I are through. Is there a problem?"

"Oh—oh, no. This is my first international fugitive hunt and I'm getting used to the rules and regulations of another country. I'm right behind you."

Kurt flashed Ashlee a warning look. He placed the black box holding the guns on the divider. She smiled coyly at the Mexican officer and took a seat against the wall. Kurt sidled through the swinging door and followed the tall man into another room. Within five minutes, he was returning through the swinging door to the reception area. Officer Mendoza motioned for Ashlee to follow him.

"Don't blow it," Kurt muttered as they passed.

She graced him with a sickly sweet smile. "Don't worry about me. Worry about yourself."

She disappeared behind the door.

~ * ~

Once the door closed, Officer Mendoza walked around an immense, ornate wood desk to a wooden armed chair with tapestry upholstery. He slid the chair to the corner of the room and, standing on the seat, adjusted a camera to point at the ceiling.

"What the...?" The lieutenant, placing his finger over his lips and shaking his head, halted Ashlee from further conversation.

The lieutenant climbed down from the chair and moved it behind the desk. He carefully walked to a picture mounted on the wall of a man astride a horse. He slid his fingers down the side, stopping in the middle, and pulled a small black nub from the frame. Checking over several items, he retrieved half a dozen of the round nubs. He dumped them into an ashtray and placed the ashtray in front of a radio situated on one corner of his desk. He turned it on and increased the volume. Ashlee put her hands over her ears as the eardrum-splitting music saturated the room.

Walking to the front of the desk, the lieutenant took Ashlee's hand and walked her to the furthest corner of the room, where he gathered her into his arms and kissed her passionately.

"I have waited twenty years for that kiss. What took you so long, *chato*?" He squeezed her to him.

Ashlee leaned into the muscular chest and, closing her eyes, inhaled the subtle smell of cinnamon. She drew a finger over the cotton material that stretched over his bulging biceps. "Timing, Raul, timing. It took longer for things to come together than I expected."

"Who is this gringo you travel with? He is not your *amor*, is he?"

"Good lord, no. He is convenient, useful, and disposable."

She raised her cool blue eyes and found his dark olive ones surveying her. The rich warmth of his face invited caresses. Ashlee gave in to her urge and reached up to caress him. Raul caught her hand in his and, turning it palm side up, he placed a delicate kiss in the middle. Ashlee felt her knees begin to buckle.

"Raul, you know how that unhinges me. I don't think I can control myself. If you don't stop now, I'll be forced to ravish you right here," she warned him huskily.

"Well, *mi amor*, then we will set a time to complete this—conversation." He kissed her forehead. "But it is important you hold on to an item for me."

"What?"

He reached into his shirt pocket and retrieved a key. Holding it at her eye level, he continued. "This is the key to our place. I will come to your hotel tonight and explain." He pressed the key into her palm and, closing her fingers around it, he kissed each finger.

They lingered for a moment longer, the body sensations overwhelming them.

Raul placed a quick kiss on Ashlee's cheek then moved toward the ashtray on his desk. He picked up the microphones and replaced them. As he passed the desk, he lowered the radio and gestured for Ashlee to sit in the chair in front. Once again, he pulled the chair to the corner of the room and repositioned the camera before taking a seat behind the massive wooden desk.

"When did you leave America, Officer Madison?" he asked.

"We discovered the prisoner missing from her hospital bed around ten o'clock last night. A search of her apartment turned up an itinerary for a trip to Mazatlán leaving this morning at three a.m. After reporting the escape to our office, we traveled to the airport where we boarded a plane at about five a.m.," she said.

"Do you believe it is necessary to carry your weapons to find this fugitive?"

Placing his elbows on the arms of the chair, he templed his fingers in front of him and rested his chin on the top.

"I do, Lieutenant. She has attempted murder twice before and has no qualms about shooting anyone who gets in her way. I believe we have an obligation to arm ourselves to locate her as quickly as possible, and return her back to America to stand trial for her crimes," she said.

"Frankly, I agree. If there is anything my department can do to assist you, please contact me." He picked up a business card that had lain on the desk and handed it to Ashlee. She noted his handwriting on the backside and, casually turning her back to the camera, she flipped the card over: "Holiday Inn, Av. Camarón Sabálo, seven-thirty."

"Thank you, Lieutenant. If there is anything we need, I'll call."

They shook hands and Officer Mendoza walked her out to the barrier, opening the swinging door to let her through.

~ * ~

Kurt noted the smug look on Ashlee's face as she emerged from the lieutenant's office. *I hate to think what that smile means, however, if I know Ashlee, she's got the Mexican cop eating out of her hand. We need that right now.*

Ashlee walked out and past Kurt toward the exit, trailing the light scent of cinnamon behind her. Kurt sniffed and glared at her. The sergeant shut the box and handed Kurt his weapons, at the nod of approval from Officer Mendoza.

She turned, her hand on the door handle, and thanked the clerk and lieutenant. With one quick move, she opened the door and was out in the hallway before Kurt could react. He nodded to the officials as he clutched the weapons in his hands and scurried out the door.

The clerk at the desk smirked as he said to Raul. "*El Americano no tienes huevos*, no?"

A look of concern quickly crossed the lieutenant's face. "You're right, Erasto, he has no backbone."

## Twenty

"Ashlee! Where the hell are we going?" Kurt fell into step alongside her.

"To catch the bus to town."

"How do you know about the bus to town?" Kurt shot her a sidelong glance.

"I asked the Lieutenant before I left his office. It seemed the logical thing to do."

She stopped abruptly. Fisting her hands on her hips, she turned to him. "What is your problem? Since we checked in to the security office, you've been acting like some teenage boy with a jealous crush. I'm trying to make our presence here as unobtrusive as possible, but you keep acting like some kind of injured lover."

"I thought we were in this together," he said.

"We are."

"Then why does it seem like you're trying to seduce every man we see? And why didn't you tell me you spoke Spanish? I looked like an idiot back there." Kurt's face was beginning to flush as his voice was becoming louder.

"Look." Ashlee unclenched her fists and put a hand on Kurt's arm. "I'm sorry if it seems like I'm playing the temptress, but we're in a culture where men believe women can't do jobs such as that of a police officer. So, I play to what they believe. We get information and don't raise any suspicions. I didn't tell you about speaking Spanish because, quite simply, I didn't realize you didn't know. How about I give you a brief update while we walk to catch the bus?"

He nodded.

"I was an exchange student in my sophomore year of high school. It was the last year my dad was around and we had the money and connections, so I could choose anywhere I wanted to go. I chose to go to Mexico. In fact, I spent the year here in Mazatlán."

Kurt stopped in his tracks and stared at Ashlee. "So that's how you know about the transportation systems here."

"Yes, that's how I know about the bus and working with the local authorities, and men's attitudes toward women, and a lot of other things. That's also why my Spanish is so good. Now you have all the details, shall we catch the bus? The next one won't be along for another hour and I don't want to take any chances that Corey Williams will show up and take me back to that hellhole called Oakdale."

They stepped into the tropical afternoon. Heat waves shimmered up from the sidewalks and roadways in front of the terminal, but the breeze, tinged with a floral sweetness and jet fuel, gave a false sense of coolness. Ashlee spotted the line for the bus into town and quickly stepped to board. Kurt followed, realizing just how warm the afternoon was when he felt the trickle of sweat down his chest as soon as they'd boarded the bus and were on their way to downtown Mazatlán. The effort made by the bus air conditioner was lost on the crush of humanity traveling the twenty minute ride into town. Most appeared to be locals heading home from work, but there were a few pale, excited faces in the crowd. Kurt had lost visual contact with Ashlee and began to worry. The bus pulled up in front of the Holiday Inn on Avenue Camarón Sabálo and stopped. A voice behind him spoke.

"This is our stop. Push your way out."

Kurt complied, pushing and squeezing through the throng, nearly falling out of the crowded bus onto the sidewalk. Taking a moment to catch his breath, he turned to see Ashlee gazing at the façade of the hotel.

"You okay?" he asked.

"I'm fine. Just brings back some good memories." Ashlee strode forward to the entrance of the hotel. She rented two rooms using Elaine Madison's credit card and identification. When the clerk handed her the keys, she tossed one to Kurt.

"For the next twenty-four hours, I don't care what you do. Just leave me alone. I want to sleep in a decent bed and take a long bath—alone. If I need to contact you, I know which room you're in, so I'll call you." She turned to leave. "By the way, there are several shops along the main street that stay open until ten o'clock tonight. You might want to buy a change of clothes to blend in a little better. There's also a McDonald's down the block." She turned on her heel and disappeared out the front entrance.

Kurt followed her example and, after a short walk in the warm floral tinged ocean air, he spied a clothing store featuring men's fashions in the window. Twenty minutes later, he emerged with a bagful of new clothing. He ambled along the sidewalk enjoying the feel of the evening breeze on his face. The fresh air revitalized him, and he continued until he located the McDonald's where he ordered a plain American cheeseburger with small French-fries, pulling out the twenty-dollar bill he'd confiscated from Ashlee. *I may be able to adjust to living here, after all. As long as I can get a Mickey D's once in a while, I'll survive.*

He smiled as he gathered his belongings from the table and headed back to the hotel. Double checking the number on his key, he took the elevator to the second floor and located his room. Inside, Kurt dropped the sacks of clothing on the floor and sat on the bed. He picked up the phone and instructed the front desk that he was not to be disturbed for the next twenty-four hours. The clean shirt he had pulled out of his closet last night was sweat stained and peeled off his body. *All I want is a shower.*

Slipping out of his clothing, Kurt strolled into the mosaic-tiled bathroom and indulged himself. He grabbed the fluffy white towel from the rack and buffed his body dry until his skin glowed pink. Feeling clean and with his stomach full, his only thoughts were of uninterrupted sleep. A quick flick of the light switch and within five minutes Kurt was softly snoring.

~ * ~

Ashlee sat on the side of the tub and swirled her hand through the warm bathwater. Taking the bath salts provided by the hotel, she poured them into the filling tub and stepped into the warm fragrant bath. Sliding in and allowing the fragrant concoction to cover her up to her neck, she sighed deeply. *I've been waiting for this for weeks.*

She lay there until her fingertips began to wrinkle. Grudgingly, she lifted her foot out of the silky water and flipped the lever of the stopper with her toe. When the water had drained from the tub, she engaged the shower, soaping her body and shampooing her hair. Standing under the sluicing water, she allowed her tension to swirl down the drain. With a flick of her hand, the healing water stopped and she stepped onto the clean thick bathmat, dripping slightly as she wrapped a towel about her head to form a turban. With a second towel, she patted herself dry and tied the ends together forming a loose shift. Padding into her room, Ashlee stopped to admire the beautiful turquoise sheath she had chosen for the evening. It would accent her eyes and still be comfortable enough to sit through dinner. She glanced into the mirror and found a smile beginning to grace her lips. *It's been a long time since I've felt this giddy.* She fingered the material. *I doubt I'll have it on much longer after we've eaten.*

This evening had been twenty years in the planning. Humming a tune learned as a child, Ashlee slipped the shift over her damp hair and down her lithe body as she put her makeup on with the utmost of care. Those people who'd called her heartless just didn't know where her heart was being held hostage.

The phone rang with two angry bursts.

"Hello?"

"Señorita, we have a meal on its way to your room. We wished to make sure it was something you were expecting?"

"Yes. *Muchas gracias*."

"*Bueno. Pase un buen noche*; have a good evening."

Ashlee had no sooner hung up the phone when there was a knock on the door. She glanced through the peephole. A young Mexican gentleman in the room service uniform stood behind a covered cart. Ashlee ushered the young man in and he steered the cart next to the table before, upon being generously tipped, he left the room, telling the "Señorita" if she needed anything to please ask for Vincínco.

Ashlee lifted the cover from the food and was enveloped in the smell of melted cheese, red sauce and grilled chicken. Her stomach protesting, she quickly covered the food. Rummaging through the bags she had set on the floor after shopping, she retrieved a bottle of wine. She took out the corkscrew she'd purchased and opened the wine, allowing it to breathe. As she was pulling out the stemmed glasses, there was a quiet knock on her door. Ashlee stopped and held her breath. Then the knocking began again in a series of two swift raps. She dashed to open the door.

Raul Mendoza stood before her, his dazzling smile blinding against the cinnamon glow of his face. "Miss Elaine Madison? I have some further questions I wish to ask. May I come in?"

Ashlee grabbed his arm and yanked him inside the room to her arms. After kicking the door shut, she mashed his lips to hers. His tongue gently pushed for entry, and she welcomed him, groaning as the sensations washed over her body. He slipped his arms around her waist and pulled her to his body, revealing his growing need for her. His hand slipped from her waist to her breast. He let his fingers roam over the hardened nipple then, hooking his thumb under her strap, he moved the material from her shoulder down her arm. The top of her breast heaved and shook with desire as he slipped his hand under the light material. Fingers played over silky fragrant skin and Ashlee pushed her breast into his warm hand.

She extricated her mouth from his and asked huskily, "Do you want to have dinner first or make love?"

Raul's eyes roved over Ashlee's exposed breast, taking in the hardened rosy nipple. He licked his lips and moved to her bud, his tongue dancing over the taut skin as Ashlee moaned. He pulled it into his warm mouth and sucked hard, catching her when her knees buckled. He lifted her shift and pulled her against his hard member, feeling her moistening crotch dampen the material of his slacks.

"Let's eat before the food grows cold. We'll have dessert later."

His thumb moved over her nipple one more time as he moved the strap back up to her shoulder.

"Ooooo… you tease!" Ashlee grinned, disentangling from his arms and walking to the table. Pouring two glasses of wine, she held one out to him. Raul took the glass and raised it to her.

"To my first and only love. Now we are together, let nothing come between us."

They touched rims and took a sip. Ashlee prepared the plates with the sumptuous food. The aromas set her taste buds to tingling. "I thought we could eat out here."

They sat quietly, eating and gazing at each other.

"Raul?"

"Hmmm?"

"What about your wife and children?"

"Nothing will change, my love. As I wrote and told you years ago, this is a marriage of convenience and money. My wife, Leticia, is a good woman who has raised our children well, serves as a companion to official functions and parties, and will tolerate any indiscretion I commit as long as she has my name and status in the community. Divorce is out of the question. But you, my darling, will always be the one I love. You stole my heart when we were children, and I have never given it to anyone else. You, I cherish." Raul stood and offered his hand.

Ashlee was drawn into his dark gaze. She took his proffered hand and rose from the table. He led her to the bedroom and laid her across the bed.

Two hours had lapsed since Raul and Ashlee lay down. Against his bare chest, she listened to the sound of his gentle breathing. She watched as his taut stomach rose and fell with each breath. She fingered the downy, soft black hair that ran from his chest to beneath his bellybutton. He started and gently moved her head to a pillow, as he slung his legs over the side of the bed. With a proficient move he was into his clothes and heading into the bathroom.

Ashlee raised herself up on her elbow. *What just happened here? I've waited for this night for over twenty years and this is it? It can't be.*

Raul emerged from the bathroom. "What is the matter, my love? You look confused."

"Frankly, I am. I've waited for us to be together, to make love, for over twenty years, and you're acting like I'm a paid hooker. I'm very confused, Raul. You're the one who kept writing and phoning me to come back to Mexico. Well, here I am and, if this is the way things are going to be, you can just forget about us. I could've stayed in the US for treatment like this."

Ashlee stormed past him to the bathroom.

He grabbed her wrist and pulled her to him, crushing her lips against his. His hand wandered down her naked body and found the moist warm point between her legs. He gently began to manipulate her sensitive spot. She moaned and pushed into him. Slowly, he pulled his lips from hers.

"I can't spend the amount of time with you I wish tonight. But it's just the beginning. We'll have the rest of our lives to make love and be together. Think about it, sweetness. If, for any reason, someone spotted me entering, the longer I stay the less likely it is they'll believe our business is official. We don't want someone beginning to investigate, do we?"

Ashlee pushed her body against Raul's.

"Again, you're right. But I've never felt so good and, frankly, I don't want it to end."

"Neither do I, my love—neither do I. But it must."

Raul slid away and into the bathroom to wash his hands. Ashlee stood uncertainly, trying to decide what to do. She and Raul exchanged places and as she started to shut the bathroom door his hand shot out, holding it open.

"Do you remember the summer cottage my parents used to take us to for a day at the beach?"

"The one at Tuxpan?" she replied.

"Teacapán. The cottage at Tuxpan is the one my family and I now use. The key I gave you earlier will get you into the cottage at

Teacapán. There has been some building going on by Americans so you do have some neighbors close by, but it's still pretty isolated. The little grocery store in the town has an account in the name we chose, Alicia Gonzalez. I informed the clerk you were the American cousin that used to visit in the summertime and would be staying indefinitely. You should have no problems. The bills will be sent to me, and you and I can arrange their payment. If you need anything, call me at the office." He opened his wallet and extracted a business card that he handed to Ashlee.

Raul then leaned into the bathroom and kissed her deeply. He broke the kiss and let his hand linger on her exposed breast. She closed her eyes, savoring the sensation. A slight breeze across her nipple snapped her eyes open. Raul was gone. She hadn't even heard the door close. Ashlee sagged against the counter. This was not what she had hoped would happen, but Raul was right. They needed to maintain a low profile until she could find a way to dispose of Kurt.

*I'll take a shower and crawl into bed. Maybe a little television and sleep will help me find a solution to this problem. It can't be any tougher than getting rid of Thomas Manning... just more permanent.*

## Twenty-one

Riona jerked awake. She felt sweat trickling between her breasts and her hands were clammy as she pushed the stray hair from her face. She signaled the stewardess.

"Yes, miss?"

"Let me have a shot of your best vodka." Riona pulled her seatback upright and pointed the fan to blow directly on her. She pulled out her money and exchanged a ten dollar bill for the miniature bottle of alcohol the flight attendant handed her. Waving away the change the attendant tried to hand her, she opened the bottle and drained the contents. The dragons dive bombing her stomach began to settle down as the warmth of the alcohol spread over her body. *I thought I'd gotten over André—maybe not.*

She turned and looked at Corey's rugged face. He seemed to have finally relaxed. A gentle snoring was emitting from his lips, causing them to purse slightly as he blew out air. She gazed at his tanned high cheekbones. They emphasized eyes she knew were lusciously hazel, changing with his moods. At the moment his eyes were closed, but the long dark lashes curling against his face were thick enough to make any woman jealous. She leaned over and lightly ran her finger down his ruggedly square jaw line. Stubble was beginning to appear, rubbing rough against her finger. Full lips beckoned for her touch but she resisted the urge to caress them. *Damn his lips look kissable. I ought to just kiss him, but he'd probably have a heart attack.*

Riona smiled at her mischievousness. The overhead air started to hiss as the plane began its descent and the cabin pressure adjusted. Using a trick taught her by her scuba diving instructor, she held her nose and blew to relieve the force pushing against her eardrums, smiling as they crackled and popped.

Corey stirred. His eyes opened slowly and focused on the back of the seat in front of him. He narrowed his brows. *Where the hell am I?* Focusing his eyes and brain, the heaviness on his inner ears reminded him with each building moment he was inside a plane. He yawned and felt immediate relief.

"Well, how are you feeling?" Riona asked.

"All right. I'll feel a hell of lot better when I get on the ground and in a real bed. I'm getting too old to stay up for twenty or thirty hours at a time. This time zone hopping is for the birds. I hope we'll be able to pick up a trail on Ashlee and Kurt fairly easily. I'm really in no mood to go tromping around Mexico looking for them, but I promised Justin and Diane that Ashlee would serve her time."

The intercom overhead clicked to life and a disembodied voice announced the flight was approaching Mazatlán and everyone would need to buckle seat belts and get ready for landing.

Corey and Riona readied themselves as the plane began to bump and toss.

"You'd think they'd be able to make this landing thing smoother," grumped Corey.

"It's the mountains," Riona answered.

"What?"

"Mountains cause a change in the currents making the air above them turbulent; consequently the ride resembles a roller coaster." Riona cinched her seat belt.

"Where do you come up with this stuff?" Corey looked at her in amazement.

"When you travel over the world in one of these things you pick up lots of unnecessary trivia about flying, and you either get used to it or drink. I chose to adjust."

Corey grumbled and tightened his seat belt. *You owe me so much, Justin. Next time I'm sending one of the younger detectives.*

The plane bumped on the runway and slowly taxied to the exit ramp. Riona and Corey sat in their seats, observing as the plane emptied of flushed faced tourists excited to begin their weeklong vacation. They rose and, approaching the flight attendant, Corey flashed his badge.

"Miss? I need to retrieve my weapon from the Captain's locker. Will you get him for me?"

The flight attendant disappeared into the cockpit and emerged with the co-pilot. He carried a black box in his hands.

"Identification, please."

Corey pulled his badge and ID tag from his pocket and handed them to the co-pilot.

After carefully examining both pieces, the co-pilot handed them back. He released the box to Corey.

"Enjoy Mazatlán."

"Thanks."

Corey and Riona moved up the exit ramp. The oily smell of jet fuel seeped into small openings between the partitions and mixed with a sweet heady scent of native flora, creating a distinctive perfume. Once in the terminal, the two stepped to the side allowing the crew to pass them. Corey stood and closed his eyes.

"Getting your land legs?" Riona allowed a small smile to play across her lips.

Corey nodded and pulled cool air into his lungs. It lacked the recycled staleness of the air inside the plane's cabin. He opened his eyes and relaxed his shoulders.

"I'm feeling much better now. Let's find the security office and check in. Once we get ourselves registered, we can find a hotel and relax. I could really go for a hot shower."

The two sauntered down the airport corridor in the direction most of the travelers seemed to be heading. It opened into a large terminal with overhead reader boards showing incoming and outgoing flights in Spanish and English. A podium map of the airport layout stood centrally located in an area dotted with shops that were selling every imaginable item a traveler could desire. Corey quickly located the security offices on the map and, nodding to Riona, he moved in that direction. He smiled as he passed coffee shops featuring Starbuck's coffee, fast food eateries with familiar American names, and newsstands featuring papers from the largest cities in the US. The only indication he was no longer on American soil was the prevalence of spoken Spanish.

Opening the door to the security office, Corey was struck by the quiet. Compared to the din in the outer corridors, the hushed atmosphere resembled a city library. A single female clerk in an airport security uniform sat behind an ancient desk, typing furiously on a computer keyboard. She looked up when Corey cleared his throat.

"Excuse me, miss. Do you speak English?" he asked.

"No."

"Damn. Now what do I do?" He turned to Riona, furrowing his brows and frowning.

She stepped to the counter and spoke to the clerk in Spanish. "Excuse me, miss? How can you know what he said if you don't speak English?"

The clerk looked up at Riona and reddened.

She stuttered, "I have a report I must complete. Can you wait about five minutes?"

"No problem."

Riona turned to Corey and repeated to him in English, "We'll need to hold on for about five minutes or so. Have a seat." She indicated the old wooden chairs pushed against the wall.

The two sat and, as promised, five minutes later the clerk got up from her desk and stood at the counter. In textbook English, she asked, "How may I help you?"

Corey sputtered, looking at Riona in astonishment.

They approached and set the black box on the counter.

"Yes, I would like to register my weapon." Corey pulled out his badge and the gun registration from inside his pocket. "We're in Mexico to locate a felon I believe has fled to your city. Have you had any other officers from this location check in with you?"

Corey pushed his identification tag from Oakdale police department toward the clerk. She picked it up and read.

"You know, I believe we had a couple officers check in earlier today. Let me get our logbook." She moved to her desk and pulled a tattered book from several held between bookends on her desktop. Flipping through several pages, she stopped and ran her finger down the page.

"Yeah, here it is. A Kurt Lee and Elaine Madison from Oakdale Police Department checked in earlier. They registered their weapons because they said they were looking for an Ashlee Anderson. They even left us a poster to put up."

The clerk pulled a poster from the top tray of her in-box. She walked it over to Riona and Corey and slid it across the counter top. In an exact duplicate of official wanted posters was a picture of Elaine Madison. All the information and the name under the picture were for Ashlee Anderson. The phone number given as the official contact point was Kurt Lee's private cell phone number. Corey and Riona exchanged looks.

"He's in this up to his neck, isn't he?" Riona asked him.

"Looks like it." He shook his head sadly.

"Did they happen to mention where they might be heading, or a hotel where they might be spending the night?" He looked at the clerk hopefully.

She nodded her head negatively. "Sorry, no mention in the log, but most Americans stay at the Holiday Inn on the Camarón Sabaló on the Zoná Dorada. Any of the taxi drivers can take you there. Is there anything else I can do for you?"

"Yeah, can you give me a permit to carry my weapon while I'm here? It's only going to be for two weeks. If I can't find my fugitive in two weeks, I'll hand the search over to the federal authorities and let them do the footwork." Corey snapped open the black box to reveal his police revolver.

The clerk picked up the revolver, examined the chamber, and sited down the barrel. She put the gun back into the case and went to the desk. Retrieving several pieces of paper from her drawers, she came back to the counter and filled out a form which she slid to Riona.

Riona read the Spanish and translated for Corey. He signed in the appropriate spots and, pocketing his copy, picked up the weapon box.

"Let's find a hotel and call it a day. I'm hungry and desperately want a shower."

Riona agreed and, thanking the clerk, the duo left the security office.

The clerk walked back to the desk and opened her top drawer. She retrieved a small black book and thumbed through the pages until she'd found the number she was searching for. She pulled her cell phone out of her purse and dialed. The line was answered after the second ring.

"I really hate to interrupt your evening, sir, but two Americans—one was a police officer—were just here asking about the other Americans that came in earlier. Seems they're looking for the same fugitive. I told them I didn't know where the other officers were staying, but mentioned most of the Americans stay at the Holiday Inn. I thought you should know, sir. Yes, sir. Goodnight, sir."

The clerk slipped her phone into her purse with a smile. Maybe she'd be able to get a different shift now. Her work hours were causing problems with her marriage, but this job paid better than working in the family restaurant and gave her time away from her jealous husband. Maybe they'd move her to the day shift. She could only hope.

## Twenty-two

Corey and Riona stood on the pavement outside the airport terminal.

"According to the bus schedule, we've got about ten minutes until the next one comes by here. It will take us into the Golden Zone, as it's called, where we can find a car rental place and get some transportation. I like knowing I'll get where I want to be on time, my time, instead of the local time." Riona led Corey to the curb, and when the bus arrived she pulled out some coins and paid both fares.

"Where'd you get local money?" he asked.

"There are kiosks all over the airport that will exchange money from dollars to local currency and from local currency to dollars. It's all about knowing."

Corey nodded. He watched out the window as the landscape whizzed past. The fifteen mile drive from the airport to the Zoná Dorado took half an hour because of the constant stopping of the city bus. The couple stepped to the concrete and started walking. Within a city block, they'd passed three car rental places and finally decided to use one familiar to Riona.

At the rental desk, she turned to him and asked, "Have you driven outside the US?"

"No." He shifted his gaze to the floor.

"Well, I have and I've got an international license, so I'll have to rent the car as well as drive. You can reimburse me later, okay?"

He nodded and crossed his arms.

Once Riona had completed the paperwork, and been given instructions in Spanish, the blue sedan they were assigned was driven up to the curb for them. Inside the vehicle, Riona adjusted the seat, pulled the map from the glove box, and handed it to Corey.

"You navigate and I'll pilot. I understand it's not in the male nature to read maps, but this is an exception to the rule, and I promise I won't tell anyone." Riona's smile made Corey grin.

"I suspect blackmail is illegal even in Mexico." He opened the map and turned it in the right direction. "We're within two blocks of the Holiday Inn that the clerk in the security office mentioned. It appears they have a parking lot out front. Why don't we go over there and see if we can surprise Kurt and Ashlee?"

"Sure. One detail—which direction do I need to point the car?" Riona raised her eyebrows.

"Smart ass. Pull out from the curb and continue in the same direction for two blocks. I suspect the sign on the other side of the street will be readable in Spanish as well as in English. At that point, turn left into the parking lot, find an unoccupied place, pull the car into the parking place then put the vehicle in park," he said.

"My but we're a bit touchy, aren't we?"

"Tired and jet lagged. If we don't find Kurt and Ashlee at the Holiday Inn, let's see if we can get a room. If we can't get one there, I'm going to continue to be touchy until we've stopped moving for at least a half hour. Once we stop moving and I've had a decent meal, I may, and I said *may*, stop being cranky. No guarantees."

Riona laughed and glanced sideways at him. She was beginning to feel comfortable, and it scared her. She spotted the familiar sign, as per Corey's instructions, and parked the rental vehicle.

The couple exited the car and went inside the hotel. The lobby stretched before them as they went to the check in desk.

"*Bueños noches, Señores. Como está?* How are you this evening?" The clerk smiled at the pair.

"We're fine, thank you. We've just flown in to meet our friends and they neglected to give us their room numbers. Would you be so kind as to let us know which rooms they're staying in, so we may join them?"

Corey looked so earnest Riona ached to laugh.

"I'm sorry, sir, but it is against our policy to give out room numbers to anyone except the specific guest staying in that room." The friendliness had disappeared and was replaced by irritated haughtiness. She started to turn toward the mail slots.

"Excuse me, Miss?" Corey had pulled out his badge and laid it on the counter.

"I believe they're listed as officers Kurt Lee and Elaine Madison. Their room numbers?"

Her face draining of color, the clerk turned the computer screen toward her and typed in the two names.

"Mr. Lee is in room two twenty-three and Ms. Madison is in suite six twenty-three. Would you like me to ring them for you?" Her lips quavered slightly as she smiled.

"No, thank you. They're expecting us—I'm surprised they didn't leave a message here at the desk—so we'll just go on up." Corey pulled his badge back and replaced it in his pocket.

Gently sliding his hand under Riona's arm, he guided her to the elevator. They stood looking up at the dial. Once inside the elevator, Corey turned to Riona.

"Kurt or Ashlee first?" he said.

"Who do you want more?" she answered.

"Ashlee, definitely." Corey's jaw tightened.

Riona pushed the sixth floor button. As the doors silently opened, Corey and Riona stepped out. They moved down the corridor with stealth and found suite six twenty-three.

Corey turned to Riona. "You ready?"

She nodded. He knocked on the door.

## Twenty-three

Raul Mendoza swore as he snapped shut his cell. He'd only been home for an hour and his wife was already giving him grief because of his earlier appointment.

"Now what?" She eyed him.

"It's official business, my love. That was the office at the airport. I must go out, and I'm not sure how long I'll be gone."

He got up from the couch and moved to the bedroom to change. *If this is an indication of how things are going to be with Ashlee around, I'm not sure I want to put up with it.*

He changed into his uniform and strapped on his revolver. Double checking his appearance in the mirror, he walked through the hallway into the living room. He kissed his wife's cheek and went out the front door to the police cruiser parked in his driveway. Getting in, he turned on the radio and backed out into the street. Glancing back at his home, he noticed the curtains draw aside and his wife peer out the front room window. This situation was going to be tenuous at best but, hell, he'd been able to juggle two women before, and this wasn't a new adventure for him. He put his wife out of his mind and, flipping on the overhead lights, sped to the hotel.

The drive, with his lights flashing all the way, took him only ten minutes. He switched the lights off a block before the inn and silently slid into a parking place out front. He'd take Ashlee and her escort to the beach house personally. Only then could he guarantee she'd be in place, and there'd be no danger of her contacting his wife. Raul moved directly to Ashlee's room and pounded on the door. It took two tries, but she finally answered.

"Back for more? Come on in." She opened the door and ambled to a chair at the table, grabbing a cigarette and her lighter. She lit up and blew smoke into the air.

"Get your stuff. We've got to get you and your friend to the beach house, *now*!" Raul strode to the closet and began pulling clothes from the rod, tossing them on the bed.

"What is your problem?" Ashlee yelled, snubbing out her cigarette and pushing out of the chair. She dashed to the closet.

"Stop it!" She yanked the clothes from Raul's hands.

Raul grabbed her wrists.

"Two Americans came into the office less than an hour ago and questioned the clerk about you and your policeman boyfriend. She let them know you were in Mexico and, while she didn't tell them where you were staying, she did mention most Americans stay at this hotel. I figure we have about an hour at best to get you to the cottage on the beach. Now, do you want to stand here and argue, or get the hell out of town?"

Ashlee threw the clothes on the bed and pulled a large bag from the garbage can where she'd thrown it earlier. She stuffed the clothes into the bag and emptied every drawer in the room. Pulling on a pair of jeans and a peasant style blouse she'd purchased, she slipped her feet into her huarache sandals and headed to the door with Raul close on her heels. The two descended to Kurt's floor and pounded on his door.

When five minutes of knocking brought no response, Raul enlisted a passing bellboy to open the door by flashing his official identification. Once inside the two quickly got the sleepy Kurt up and packed. They cut off his questions and hustled to the police cruiser parked out front. Raul opened the trunk and threw in the bags of clothing. He escorted Ashlee to the front seat and placed Kurt in the back seat behind the mesh screen.

They sped through town with lights and sirens blazing. Once out of town, Raul turned the lights and siren off, slowing the cruiser to legal speed.

Kurt could no longer contain his curiosity. "All right, I've got to know what's going on here. Why the hell are you, a Mexican official, so willing to help Elaine and me in our search for the fugitive we're looking to find?"

Raul glanced at Ashlee and in the rear view mirror at Kurt.

"First, Officer Lee, I'm aware that the woman you keep referring to as Elaine Madison is Ashlee Anderson."

Even in the dark, Raul could see the color drain from Kurt's face.

"The scenario has changed in the last hour, and our timetable has to be moved ahead sooner than we anticipated. Ashlee and I have known each other since we were teenagers and she was an exchange student living with my family. She was my first love and I hers. We've always kept in touch, first with writing, then emailing as the technology progressed. When she first sensed she might be facing problems in Virginia, we formulated the plan you've been executing. The only change is that we need to move up the events to benefit us, not your adversary. Does that answer your question?" Raul's dark eyes stared at Kurt.

"Yeah." He slumped back in the seat.

~ * ~

Corey knocked for the third time and the response was the same—no answer.

"Let's try Kurt's room. Maybe they've decided to stay there for the night." He strode toward the elevator, Riona matching him step for step.

"Why would they stay in one of the standard rooms when Ashlee has a suite?" she asked.

"Ashlee never does what you'd expect. The only consistent quality she has is that she's inconsistent."

Corey punched the elevator button for the second floor.

Bursting out of the elevator, Corey hustled his burly frame to the door and started pounding. Riona slid up behind him and tapped his shoulder after a couple minutes.

"It looks as though they've taken off. Why don't we go ask the desk clerk to call up to the rooms, in case, by some feat of deafness, they're actually inside and not hearing you attempting to break down the door?" Riona raised her eyebrows in question.

Corey stopped and turned toward her. "Great idea. Let's go."

They returned to the front desk and faced the same nervous clerk.

"Yes?" She gulped. Her face was still pale and she was visibly shaking.

Corey relaxed his stance and smiled. He watched as the clerk seemed to relax a little. "I'm so sorry to bother you, miss, but our friends don't seem to be answering their door. Would you mind placing a call to both rooms to see if they may have been in the shower when we knocked?"

Riona watched him smile. His eyes crinkled at the corners and a twinkle appeared. The corners of his mouth gave way to a genuine smile and his teeth were blinding in their brilliance. *If the smile doesn't melt her, she's truly the ice queen of Mexico.*

The young lady's mouth quivered slightly then returned Corey's smile. Her lovely tanned face relaxed, showcasing deep brown eyes above the tiny turned up nose and plump bowed lips.

"Certainly."

She placed a call to both rooms and stood glancing nervously about the room as the phone rang unanswered in each location.

"I'm so sorry, sir, but it appears the occupants of those rooms have stepped out. Is there anything else I can do for you?" Her perky attitude was beginning to return.

Corey glanced at Riona then asked, "Would you have two rooms available for us?"

Consulting the computer, the clerk shook her head. "I'm so sorry but we're booked. Sales convention, however, I can phone a couple of the hotels to see if anyone might have any openings. Would that work for you?" she asked.

"That would be great. Thank you." Corey said.

The clerk spent five minutes calling around and found a couple rooms she reserved for them at the Azteca Inn, a small hotel down the street. By the time she'd given them directions to their lodgings the clerk had warmed up and was flirting with Corey.

As they climbed into the rental car, Riona commented, "You sure won her over with your boyish charm."

Corey's face morphed into a crimson mask as he turned to look out the window.

They picked up their keys at the front desk and went to their separate rooms. Corey called Riona's room. "You want to have dinner in the restaurant?" he asked.

"Are they open?" she said.

"Well, if they're not I'll bet the bar is open and has food," he replied.

"Actually, I think I'm going to take a long shower and go to bed. It's been a while since I ran all over the globe and, frankly, it's taken its toll on me. Give me a ring in the morning and let's go to breakfast before we start stomping around the countryside of Mexico. Okay?" she said.

"You're on." Corey hung up.

~ * ~

Forty-five minutes and thirty-five miles later, the police car pulled into a small village with the requisite cantina, a small, family owned market with a gas station, and not much else. A couple of turns off the main highway and the cruiser glided into the driveway of a house that faced the ocean. Raul, Ashlee and Kurt climbed out and stretched limbs tightened by stress. Raul went around the back, pulling out clothing bags and dropping them on the driveway.

Ashlee closed her eyes and sucked the salty air into her lungs. "I'd forgotten how wonderful the air smells here." She opened her eyes to gaze at the lights of a boat moored two hundred feet off shore. The reflection shimmered with the gently rolling waves.

"I thought all the fishermen would be home by now," she said to Raul.

"Most of the smart ones are. That's probably a tourist who thinks it's romantic to sleep on their boat. They'll be gone by morning. I'll open up the cottage so you can put your stuff away."

He strode through the archway of the fence surrounding the house and up a terra cotta walkway between two wings of a whitewashed adobe style home. To each side of the walkway were tastefully placed barrel and ocotillo cacti. The set-in front door was of a dense dark wood and held to the building with enormous iron hinges. The porch light, resembling a ship's lantern and decorated in the cast iron style, lit up as Ashlee and Kurt grabbed their bags off the ground.

Kurt stopped for a moment near the front door and admired the mosaic tiles surrounding the entry. Below the lantern and against the whitewashed archway of the door, Delft blue tiles numbered two-five-nine-two clearly stood out. Kurt pushed open the massive door and followed Raul through the living room and down the hall, stopping in front of two doors facing each other.

"There's food and beer in the refrigerator. Give me a day or two and I'll get you transportation. Right now though, it's probably better for you to stay out of sight. Until the others get tired of looking for you and go back to America, you're in danger."

"Do you know who they are?" Kurt looked at the tanned Mexican officer.

"My guess is Corey. He swore to Justin, my ex-husband, he'd see me go to jail." Ashlee opened the door and turned to Raul. Her eyes sparkled as her voice cooed. "You staying, love?"

Kurt watched in amazement as the handsome *Federalé* snaked his hand around Ashlee's waist and slipped into the room with her. He'd never seen Ashlee respond to a man the way she did to this Raul. Opening the door to the room he was to occupy, he went inside, dumping his clothing and cell phone on the sturdy thick dresser before sitting on the mission style double bed. His head hurt, and he was getting the distinct sensation of standing on quick sand. The plan he and Ashlee had discussed was to stay away from the big cities of Mexico for as long as it took for the fuss to die down in Oakdale. After all, he and Ashlee hadn't killed Elaine; just put her out of commission for a while. He stretched out on the bed and closed his eyes. Tossing and turning, he wasn't sure how long he lay there attempting to fall asleep, when his eyes popped open and he abruptly sat up. He'd have to look out for himself. It was evident Ashlee was doing exactly that—looking out for herself.

He flipped his legs over the edge of the bed and stood up. Grabbing his phone off the dresser, he walked to the window and pushed it open. In the distance, he could hear the waves lapping against the shoreline. The night air hung heavy with the mixed scent of ocean and jasmine. A million stars twinkled against the inky blue sky and a half-moon shone a beam of light upon the reflective water. This was the closest to heaven he'd ever get. He fished his wallet from his jeans and, searching inside, he pulled out a slip of paper. Unfolding it, he squinted at the number for several minutes until he could make it out, then he dialed. The phone rang four times.

~ * ~

Corey closed his eyes and was trying to envision himself floating on a cloud. It was an exercise the therapist had given to him when he and his ex-wife were trying to keep their marriage together. It wasn't working any better now than it did then, but he was beginning to relax and give in to the urge to sleep.

On the nightstand next to the bed Corey's cell began to play Dixie. He sat up and snapped open the instrument.

"Yeah? This is Corey Williams. What do you want?" The response woke him from any thoughts of sleep. "Where the hell are you?"

## Twenty-four

Ashlee couldn't get enough of Raul. His cinnamon colored skin felt like silk beneath her fingertips, and his experienced maneuvers brought her to heights of ecstasy she hadn't dreamed existed. After making love again she allowed him to fall asleep against her. She wasn't sure if the making love or the salt air had made her thirsty but she gently slipped away to get a drink of water.

The entry to Kurt's room was open, his back facing the doorway. Ashlee would've walked past but she heard Corey's name mentioned. *What the hell is he doing?* She leaned against the hallway wall and eavesdropped on the conversation.

"Hello, Corey? This is Kurt Lee. I've really screwed up and need to talk to you. Ashlee has a whole other life down here I didn't know about, and I'm getting the distinct feeling I'm becoming a liability. I've weighed my options and decided I'd rather do jail time in the US than push up daisies or spend time in a Mexican jail. I know she's going to be pissed at me, but at least I'll be alive and breathing.

"We're holed up in a small town called Teacapán, about forty-five miles south of Mazatlán on the coast. The house, a white adobe with blue address tiles numbered two-five-nine-two next to the doorway, is two blocks from downtown on the beachside. Blue tiles surround the archway beyond the courtyard filled with cacti. I think there'll be a police cruiser parked nearby. If nobody answers when you knock, just come inside. Ashlee will probably be busy. "

"Yeah, I know I'm an idiot, but I'd rather be a live idiot than a dead accomplice. Yeah, Corey, give me hell tomorrow when you come to get me. I'd better get off the phone now. See ya then."

When she heard Kurt snap his cell phone shut, she darted past. The floating sensations from the after effects of ecstasy had slipped away with each sentence of the overheard conversation. Now, the overwhelming desire to choke the life out of Kurt replaced ecstasy. She padded barefoot to a tall square wardrobe in the dining room and opened the doors to expose a neatly hidden bar. *If memory serves me, the tequila should be here.*

Ashlee unfastened a door inside the wardrobe and revealed a bottle with the familiar figure of José Cuervo. She undid the top and took a long draw. The golden liquid burned a trail down her throat and settled in a warming pool in her stomach. She felt the glow expand over her body. She still had the desire to kill Kurt, but she would wait until she'd slept and could think clearly. She followed the shot with the drink of water she'd wanted earlier. Heading back to her room and Raul, she glared at Kurt's closed door.

*Sleep well, you worm.*

~ * ~

Kurt hung up the phone, a chill running up his spine. He whipped around to face an empty doorway. *I swear someone's out there.* He tiptoed across the room and peeked out, checking both ways, to find a vacant hallway. He closed the door and leaned against it. *Probably just my guilty imagination.*

Turning off the lights, Kurt undressed and crawled beneath the sheets. *Tomorrow back to the US.* With that thought in mind, he fell into a dreamless sleep.

## Twenty-five

Corey got up from the bed and paced the length of the room. Kurt was far too relaxed about his situation. He didn't seem concerned enough about leaving, but Corey's gut was telling him there was immediate danger. Ashlee was a viper when it came to her own safety, and if she had a hint Kurt had contacted Corey she would do something drastic, maybe even deadly.

As much as he hated losing sleep, Corey couldn't allow Kurt to be injured. He'd been a good officer until he'd been taken in by Ashlee. Sex did strange things to men's normally logical minds.

Pacing a few more minutes, Corey decided to rescue Kurt. He would wake Riona and they'd drive to the cottage on the coast, but they'd have to leave soon. He didn't want to take any chances of Ashlee finding out about the call. Kurt had also mentioned a police cruiser on site.

*What the hell is that? I sure hope Ashlee doesn't have a local in her pocket. That'll make things twice as difficult.* He stopped and took a deep breath. *One thing at a time; awaken Riona first, rescue Kurt, then worry about Ashlee and the locals.*

Corey picked up the phone and rang Riona's room.

"What?" she mumbled.

"Did I wake you?" he asked.

"Duh. Sleeping is what most people do when they go to bed. What do you want?" she grumbled.

"Kurt Lee called me," he said.

"What?"

Corey pulled the phone from his ear.

"Yeah, he seems to think his life is in danger and he wants to take his chances back in the US. Ashlee used Kurt to get her down here to Mexico, where she apparently has been maintaining a dual life. He didn't want us to come out tonight, but I have a very uncomfortable feeling if we don't get out there as soon as possible, Kurt won't be around tomorrow."

"I agree. Everything I've seen of Ashlee tells me she won't put up with disloyalty, even if her ultimate plan is to dump him first. The slightest hint he'll turn her in or leave her will get him a new lease on death. I agree with you. Give me ten minutes and we'll leave."

In less than ten minutes, Riona stood knocking at Corey's door. He grabbed his weapon box and headed out the door. They stopped at the front desk and obtained a map of the local area. Riona drove the car to the front of the hotel and picked up Corey. Sitting in the sedan with the overhead light turned on, they traced the directions Kurt had given Corey.

"You know, this looks like it would be a really nice drive during the daytime," Riona said.

"Yeah, I'm sure it would be, and maybe someday I'll get a chance to see it during the day, but right now, if you think you've got it down, let's rescue Kurt from himself," Corey said.

Riona turned the light off and they drove toward the little town of Teacapán.

The drive was quiet, each one absorbed in their own thoughts. Just outside of the village, Riona noted, "We're almost there, about five more minutes to the town."

Corey pulled the weapon box onto his lap and began assembling his revolver. He checked the action of the cylinder, hammer and trigger while it was empty, then he loaded the cylinder and put on the safety.

"Do you think we're going to need that?" Riona looked across the seat in the darkness of the car to note the grim set of Corey's jaw line in silhouette.

"Have you ever had a gut reaction about something you're headed in to?" he asked.

"Yeah, it happened to me when I was reporting in Afghanistan. Unfortunately, it didn't turn out well for me." Riona felt her throat tighten with the tears of old memories.

"Well, I've got a bad feeling about this situation. I've never seen Ashlee harm anyone, but I don't doubt that she's capable of murder. Every person who has ever crossed her has come to regret their actions. We need to get Kurt out of there. He'll testify to her planning this break and, if she ever re-enters the US, the only thing she'll get to see is the inside of a cell."

"Well, this is the town. Now where do we go from here?" Riona pulled to the side of the road. Corey extracted the map from the glove box and went over the final few directions to the cottage. Slowly, the detective and reporter drove through the streets of the small village until they saw the police cruiser parked in front of a whitewashed adobe home. Kurt had called it a cottage, but the home Corey and Riona were viewing was anything but a cottage.

"Must have lost something in the translation," muttered Corey.

"Yeah. This resembles homes on the south side of Billington," Riona said.

"Well, let's park this thing and knock on the door. Maybe this will come off smoothly without any bloodshed," Corey said.

"Right, and pigs are flying from Texas as we speak," Riona snorted.

They parked half a block away and walked to the house. A gentle breeze played with loose tendrils of Riona's hair, tickling the sides of her face. The subtle smell of jasmine tinged with ocean air drifted on the wind. As the couple approached the house, all was dark with no visible movement inside. Corey took the lead. When he'd walked up the terra cotta flagstones to the door, he knocked loudly. He tried again, but no one answered. He grabbed the handle of the door and found it to be locked. *That's strange. Kurt said it would be open.*

He leaned over to Riona and whispered, "Let's go around back."

She nodded. They walked along a waist high fence line to the back of the house, which opened out to a patio and garden. A candle encased in lantern shell was shedding a small beam of light on the back corner of the patio and garden.

"Oh, my God." Corey put his hand out to halt Riona. He reached behind his back and pulled the revolver from his belt, where he'd stashed it when they'd exited the car. He crouched in the standard police academy position for shooting.

"Stop or I'll shoot!" he shouted.

## Twenty-six

Ashlee crept quietly into the bedroom.

"Where've you been?"

The sudden sound of Raul's velvety baritone made her jump.

"Don't scare me like that!" she fussed.

"You didn't answer me. Where've you been? With your American boyfriend?"

Ashlee could see the dangerous flashing of his eyes.

"No. For the hundredth time, Kurt is not my boyfriend. He's just a means to an end. All of our lovemaking made me thirsty so I went to get a drink of water. Lucky for us I did."

"Why?"

"As I passed Kurt's room, I heard him say the name of the police detective from America who is hunting us. The little son-of-a-bitch called and cried he wants to go home. He thinks I'm just using him and when I'm done I'm going to kill him. I hadn't thought about it before, but I will now. It'll solve all our problems. We can shoot him and take his body up to the mountains for the animals to eat. It's perfect." Ashlee smiled at her brilliance.

"There's only one problem with your plan, my love," Raul sat against the headboard.

"What?" Ashlee frowned. She didn't want to hear there might be a flaw.

"What explanation do we give to the neighbors who might have seen both of you come in tonight?" A smile tugged at the corners of his mouth.

"Can't you just intimidate them? Isn't that the way it is here?" Ashlee's lip protruded in a pout.

Raul began to chuckle, a warm bubbling sound that started deep in his soul and rolled out his mouth.

"Ashlee, you've watched too many of your American TV programs. We can't *intimidate* people any more than your American police can, no matter what the movies might portray."

"Oh." Ashlee sighed and plopped down on the bed. "What will we do? Corey's supposed to show up tomorrow."

"Don't worry, my love. I'll take care of it for you."

Raul leaned over and kissed Ashlee on the forehead. He slid out of the bed and padded, bare-assed, into the bathroom. He opened the drawer of the nightstand.

"What'd you do that for?" mumbled Ashlee, eyes half shut.

"So I don't have to fumble around in the middle of the night when I need my ulcer medicine." He slid in beside her and spooned her naked body.

"I didn't know you had an ulcer." She sighed contently and wiggled in to him.

"There's a lot you don't know about me, my love, but we have plenty of time to learn."

He wrapped his arm around her, kissing the back of her head. Raul lay in this position until he felt Ashlee's deep breathing. Slowly, he pulled his arm from around her and slipped out of the bed. He reached into the nightstand drawer with his right hand, and with his left hand he took his pillow and placed it against Ashlee. She sighed and wiggled herself against it. Raul withdrew his right hand from the nightstand drawer and gently pushed the revolver against the pillow. Holding his breath and squeezing slowly, he fired the shot through the pillow and Ashlee's back.

A puff of air escaped her body before she went limp. Raul wrapped the sheet around Ashlee's body and carried her into the bathroom, placing her in the tub. He put the gun on his dresser as he grabbed the jeans and shirt Ashlee had worn into the house. He redressed her and slipped the huaraches she'd kicked off before undressing for bed on her feet.

Grabbing the gun off the dresser, he padded across the hall to the closed door and laid his ear against it. A low continuous buzzing met his ears. He tried the handle and found the door unlocked. Tiptoeing into the room, he stopped and allowed his eyes to adjust to the dim light filtering in from the hallway. Kurt, lightly snoring, lay sprawled across the bed on his stomach.

Raul picked up the pillow that Kurt had tossed on the floor in his restlessness and moved to the side of the bed. He laid the pillow on Kurt's back and fired his weapon. Standing back, he waited a moment. When there was no movement, Raul dressed the young patrolman in the jeans and shirt he had been wearing when he arrived and, struggling under the weight, picked up the body and staggered down the hallway toward the family room. He pulled open the sliding glass door with one hand, while he awkwardly balanced the increasingly heavy body on his shoulder. Outside, he dropped Kurt on the ground and returned to the house to pull Ashlee's body from the tub. Then he carried her out, dropping her next to Kurt.

Back inside, he showered the blood away and changed into his uniform. He gathered all traces of the unexpected guests into one bag, shoved the bag into the clothes hamper and went outside. He rolled Kurt on to his stomach with his head facing the beach and dragged Ashlee's body behind Kurt a few feet, turning her on her stomach as well.

Raul looked over the scene lying in front of him. Something didn't ring true. *What's missing? Oh, yeah.*

He went in to rummage through the bedroom hamper and retrieved the weapon case from inside. Opening it, he realized the weapon was assembled and primed for use. *Perfect.*

He grabbed a washcloth from the towel rack inside the bathroom, and with a clothed hand he picked up the weapon and returned to the scene on the patio. He turned, took two shots toward the house then placed the weapon in Kurt's hand, pressing his fingers over the trigger and butt. The echo from the shots and the smell of fresh gunpowder hung in the air. Pushing the washcloth into his pocket he leaned over Ashlee and brushed the hair from her face.

"I did love you, Ashlee, but I couldn't let you control me like you did every other man in your life. I will miss you."

He started to get up and froze when he heard a voice shouting at him.

"Stop right there and raise your hands, or I'll fire my weapon!"

## Twenty-seven

Raul put both hands in to the air and rose from the ground. "I'm turning around," he yelled.

"Slowly, and don't make any sudden moves," the voice shouted back to him.

Turning on his heel, Raul could identify two figures on the other side of his fence. One was crouched in the shooting position that he recognized from his days instructing at the police academy, and the other was standing still, watching him.

"I'm a Mexican Federal Police Officer. I'm going to put my left hand in my right pocket and get my identification," he yelled.

"No. Wait a minute."

He watched as the crouched figure handed the aimed gun to the second figure, who continued to aim the weapon at him. The first figure rose and climbed his fence, taking the weapon while the second figure scrambled over the divider. The two walked under the faint light on the patio and Raul realized one of them was an attractive redheaded woman. The male, a chubby, fair complexioned police officer approached him and reached into his right pocket to retrieve his identification.

The male officer flipped open his badge holder and glanced at it, then he handed it to the female. She looked at the badge and nodded to the male.

"Sorry for all the cloak and dagger, but I received a call from a fugitive we've been tracking and it came from this location. When I heard the gunshots, I automatically went into cop mode," Corey said.

"I'm going to get my badge from my shirt pocket, so you'll know who you're dealing with here." Corey reached into his pocket and handed his own identification to the officer.

"So you're an American detective." Raul handed the badge back to Corey. "Who is your companion? Another police officer?"

"Temporarily, until I get my fugitives back to the US, she's my deputy. This is Ms. Byrne."

Riona nodded at the officer and kept silent.

"Are more officers on the way? What happened here, Lieutenant Mendoza?" Corey asked.

"Well, I just arrived myself." He moved over toward the bodies.

"I received a phone call from my neighbors that there were intruders in my cottage. This is my family's summer cottage, and the neighbors have lived here for as long as I can remember. They keep an eye on things for us."

"Anyway, I had entered the house through a side door and heard a noise in our family room. I drew my weapon and yelled out for whoever was inside to halt. Moving slowly, I noted two figures escaping out the back, and I yelled again. The farthest figure turned and I saw a muzzle flash. I dropped to the floor and heard a second shot. I reacted and shot twice.

"These are the two Americans who checked in at my office, before I left work today. They produced police identification and said they were tracking a woman fugitive. When I questioned them, I discovered the female officer had spent time in Mexico many years ago. During my questioning, we spoke of my beach cottage. I must've inadvertently given her the location. I left the office for a moment and upon my return I completed my questioning. I didn't even notice if my keys were on the desk so, when they left our offices, I wasn't concerned. Now, detective, I need to contact the coroner's office and get some officers out here to investigate."

Raul went into the cottage. Riona and Corey could hear one side of the conversation as he called the local authorities. Corey turned to Riona and raised his eyebrows in question.

"He's telling them pretty much what he told us," she answered.

"Oh."

It wasn't long before the warm, peaceful night air was shredded with the sound of police alarms. Local and federal officers appeared out of the dark and soon the cottage on the beach was awash in policemen.

Riona and Corey stood to the side, watching as they turned over the bodies of Ashlee and Kurt.

"He should have worried a whole lot more than he did," Corey commented. "It might have saved his life."

Shaking his head, he took Riona's hand in his and located Lieutenant Mendoza around the front of the cottage.

"Lieutenant?"

"Yes?"

"We would like to take the bodies back to the US so their families can bury them. Can you tell me about how long it'll be before the coroner releases them?" Corey asked.

"I believe it's going to be a couple of days. Do you have a place to stay? Somewhere in Mazatlán, perhaps?" The lieutenant crossed his arms and nodded to the arriving coroner.

"Yes, we do," Corey said.

"Well, I'd suggest you go back tonight and try to get some rest. Call me later today and I'll have a better idea of the time factors involved," Raul said as he handed his business card to Corey.

"Thank you. We'll call in the morning."

"*Buenas noches*." Raul nodded his head and disappeared into the cottage, now lit up and humming with activity.

Corey and Riona got in the vehicle and drove back to Mazatlán. The inky blue sky on the eastern horizon was changing as the day began to creep up on them.

Corey turned to Riona. "I need some sleep in a real bed. I'll call you around nine and we can get some coffee. I need your feedback on what just happened. It seems too convenient to me, a lot of pieces don't fit, but I want to sleep on it first. Deal?"

"You got it," she answered. "Until nine."

## Twenty-eight

Corey left Riona and went to his room. A quickly placed call to the front desk ensured he'd be up and moving by eight thirty. As he slipped into a fitful sleep, Kurt's phone call echoed in his mind.

"Stupid son-of-a-bitch should've known Ashlee Anderson was nothing but trouble," he mumbled as sleep pulled him under.

~ * ~

A shower helped give Corey some relief from the rapidly building headache that was beginning to overtake him. He sat on his bed and called Riona's room.

"Are you ready for coffee?" he said.

"If I have to be up at this ungodly time with only a couple of hours resembling sleep, you better damn well pump me full of coffee if you want conversation. You got five minutes to get here or I'm back in bed."

The phone went dead. Corey smiled. *She's back to herself again.*

The two met in the Azteca's restaurant and ordered coffee. No conversation passed between them until they'd drunk their first cup and started on a second.

"What'd you think of the lieutenant's explanation last night?" Corey looked to Riona.

"I think it was a load of crap, but we're really in no position to prove otherwise." She sipped her coffee and picked up a menu.

"I agree. Granted, I was no fan of Ashlee's, but I don't think she deserved to be shot in the back. And Kurt, well, he was a little smart, a little late. Did you notice, while the bodies had holes in them, the clothes didn't? Seems a little strange for burglars to go around breaking into houses naked, don't you think? If you don't mind, I'll have you talk with the lieutenant. Maybe, you can clear up these little details to his story. Your ability to speak Spanish will help eliminate any translation problems. As soon as we get the timeline from the lieutenant, I'll need to call back to Oakdale and have the captain contact the families. I want to eat something before we call. Hand me a menu, please?"

The waitress appeared and the two placed their order. Slowly enjoying their food, neither spoke. With their table cleaned and coffee cups refilled, Corey pulled his cell from his belt and handed the phone with the lieutenant's business card to Riona.

She dialed the number and waited for the lieutenant to answer.

"Hello?" Raul's rich baritone reverberated over the line.

"Good morning, lieutenant. This is Deputy Riona Byrne. I'd like to ask what kind of time line we could expect before we're able to take our citizens back to Oakdale? Also, could you recommend a reputable funeral home so we might be able to ship their bodies back in caskets? One other item—when will we be receiving the report regarding their deaths?"

There was a hesitation as Raul realized Riona was speaking to him in flawless Spanish. The arrogance he felt, when he spoke back to her in English, was absent in his reply.

"I've spoken with the coroner and it will be seventy-two hours before we'll be able to release the bodies to you. We can have them taken to the Gonzalez family mortuary for preparation. To whom should I send the bill? As far as the details of the break in, well, it may take a couple of months to get all the information together. I'll make sure your department receives a copy of our report."

"Let me have Detective Williams give you the number of our captain, and he'll arrange for payment. Thank you for your help in this matter, Lieutenant Mendoza," Riona said.

"Not at all. If there is anything I can do for you, please just call me," Raul said.

Riona flipped the cell shut and handed it to Corey.

"I believe the lieutenant was extremely surprised to hear me speaking Spanish so fluently, but it worked to our advantage. He didn't sound as though he was trying to *tourist slick* me. He says it's going to take a couple months to get the details of the break-in and subsequent deaths together. He'll mail us a report at that time. You'll need to give him the number of the captain in Oakdale to make payment arrangements. We'll be able to take Ashlee and Kurt back to the US in three days. Until they release the bodies, we've got time to kill."

"I'll call the captain and give him the news. What about the shirts?" Corey said.

"What shirts?" Riona frowned at him.

"The shirts Ashlee and Kurt were wearing with no bullet holes in them."

Riona's eyebrows rose. "Do you want to question the lieutenant about dead burglars in his family home, in his state, in his country, because they didn't have holes in their shirts?"

"Well, yes and no." Corey shifted in his seat. "I want to know what really happened."

"I'm afraid this is one glaring detail you're going to have to let go, and one reality you'll have to live without knowing." Riona shrugged her shoulders. "What about my story? You promised me first crack at it."

"Give me twenty-four hours, so the captain can inform the families before it hits the papers, okay?" Corey asked.

"All right, but after twenty-four hours, I make my deadline. A deal is a deal, Mr. Williams."

Corey nodded his head.

"Since we have seventy-two hours to burn, how about we explore this town called Mazatlán? I hear there's some fantastic shopping and the beaches aren't half bad either." Riona grinned at Corey.

"I'll shop with you, but no beaches. I hate being pushed back in to the water and told to swim free."

"Spoiled sport."

Riona got up and went to pay the bill. A chill wrapped around her spine as she passed an intricately carved mirror. She stopped and glanced sideways into the mirror. The face of her André smiled sadly at her. He mouthed the word; "goodbye".

Riona dropped her wallet in shock. When she looked into the mirror again, after picking the wallet off the floor, the vision was gone. A deep sadness washed over her for a moment. *Goodbye, my love.*

She shook off the feeling. Coming back to the table, she grabbed Corey's hand.

"Let's discover Mexico, good looking." She winked at him.

Smiling, Corey followed the sensual hips leading him to the streets of Mazatlán.

Maybe, life wasn't so bad after all

## About the Author

**C. L. Kraemer**

Fantasy, Sci Fi and Mystery writer

C. L. Kraemer has been a gypsy all her life. From her military child beginnings to her might-not-get-this-chance-again attitude after she left home, she's seen most of the continental United States as well as Hawaii and Alaska.

Three contemporary romance novels *Old Enough*; *Moon in Mazatlan*, and *If Only* are being rereleased by Rogue Phoenix Press as well as *Cats in the Cradle of Civilization.*

*Healthy Homicide*, the October 2008 launch book for Rogue Phoenix Press picks up the torch in the mystery world. In February 2010, she contributed to two Valentine's anthologies at Rogue Phoenix Press: *A Valentine Anthology*, with a story titled, "Lending Library," and *A Different Kind of Valentine* with a story titled, "The Prize."

She has completed the base story for a Dragon Fantasy series, *Dragons Among Us*, which was released August 2010 by Rogue Phoenix Press and the first follow up in the series, *Dragons Among the Eagles*, released in 2011.

"Meadows of Gold" is another faerie story released by Rogue Phoenix Press in the March 2011's anthology, *A St. Patrick's Day Tale*. A third story featuring the Fae of the valley outside Eugene, Oregon, "Defying the Odds" was included in the *May Day Anthology,* May 2013. "Boots and Blades" will be included in a Christmas 2015 collection.

August 2011 saw the release of *Shattered Tomorrows*, a mystery/crime novel loosely based on the May 7, 1981 shooting at the Oregon Museum Tavern in Salem, Oregon where four lost their lives and twenty were wounded.

A motorcycle poker run is featured in her March 2013 release, *Joker's Wild* and the third in the dragon series, *Dragons Among the Ice*, is yet to be released.

For detailed information, visit her Web sites for background on her books: www.clkraemer.com

**Other books by Christie L. Kraemer**
**Available at Rogue Phoenix Press**

*Healthy Homicide*

Two murders have occurred at the Barrel Springs Day Spa. Police hurry to find the method and reason before anyone else is murdered.

MANIC READER REVIEWS says: Healthy Homicide by C.L. Kraemer is an intriguing plot driven mystery. The plot is well written and pretty much carries the whole story...

*Dragons Among Us*

In a world full of anomalies such as the platypus and self reproducing Komodo dragon, is the human race willing to accept that dragons may be real?

Sapien Draconi-human-dragon shape shifters-all over the world face this dilemma every day. The question has become life and death as their species is plagued with unexpected and unwanted shifting in the most unlikely of places.

The Ancient Ones-full-blooded dragons-can offer advice, but few seem to put forward workable solutions to the problem.

The fate of the shape shifters hangs in the balance, and an answer must be found before the Homo Sapiens find, dissect, and hunt Sapien Draconi to extinction.

*Dragons Among The Eagles*

Aleda Sable faces the toughest decision of her life--to stay in dragon form, live as a two-legged or put one foot in the human world and one talon in the dragon world.

An urgent call from her newspaper editor sends Aleda to report on an accident whose driver appears to be a dragon. Authorities have the scene locked down and aren't allowing access to anyone. Television broadcasts flash pictures of scaly legs hanging from a crashed car. However, the bodies disappear into thin air. When the stations try follow-up reports, all they find are state highway workers busily tearing up the roads.

In determining the truth of the shifter disappearances, Aleda finds the truth of her own dilemma.

*Shattered Tomorrows*

Lucy Daniels has a secret--a deeply guarded secret.

Her life was going along just fine until she accompanied her best friend, Cassie, to her attorney's suite on top of the Equitable Building in downtown Salem, Oregon.

Once inside the lawyer's office, the world turned upside down and Lucy was forced to face a demon from her past. Thirty years ago, life had been different. Lucy had discovered Prince Charming and was headed to her happily ever after.

That's when the devil intervened and because of her brush with the devil, innocent people died.

*Joker's Wild*

Four brothers raised in the Northwest.

Two choose to stay and pursue life in Oregon. Two are seduced by the promise of Hollywood.

Life throws the Palmer brothers an ugly curve when two are killed in preventable accidents. Even more upsetting is the lack of justice in the trials of the perpetrators.

The remaining brothers will find justice using a shared passion of all the participants--motorcycle poker runs.

*Cats in the Cradle of Civilization*

Glenda Nagel, editor for Getty Museum’s monthly magazine loves her home in the Juniper Hills and her cats. When an ivory and emerald statuette of the cat goddess Bastet makes its way to her home and sets her cats on edge, Glenda is panicked.

Who knows about his and why has the darkly handsome, new Director of Egyptian Antiquities become so determined to visit her high desert home? Doesn’t Egypt have enough sand?

**C. L. Kraemer**

is also featured in these anthologies available at

Rogue Phoenix Press

*A Different Kind of Valentine*

A collection of four short stories:

*Witness* by k. J. Dahlen

When Colten finds an injured woman the police are looking for her, should he trust his own judgment about keeping her hidden from the law even if it means she might kill him?

*The Prize* by C. L. Kraemer

A computer geek learns valuable life lessons when he is given his dream car as well as a condo and the perfect job.

*Crazy 'bout You* by Clay Renick

Can a psychologist and a romance writer find true love in time for Valentines Day?

*Time Changes* by Nicolette Zamora

Laurie is just about ready to give up on love when she spies Rob Hender, her high school sweetheart's older brother.

*A St. Patrick's Day Tale*
by
Christine Young, C. L. Kraemer, Genene Valleau

Tumble through time…

…to Ireland in 1817, when tensions are high between Protestants and Catholics and fae people guide the fate of villagers. A lovely Catholic lass stumbles upon the weakly ritual fisticuffing between Irish lads. She falls into the lap of a handsome young Protestant. Family ties, grudges, and two conniving faeries threaten their budding love. But the faeries outsmart themselves when they hijack a time machine that has mysteriously appeared in their forest and are whisked to…

…Eugene, Oregon in the 20$^{th}$ century, amid a property feud between the local faeries and night elves. The conniving faeries from Olde Ireland try to stir up more mischief. However, a warrior gnome convinces the magic folk to control their own destiny, and forces the intruding faeries to take refuge in the time machine again, spinning their way toward…

…A modern day castle in western Oregon. An eccentric inventor is determined to reclaim his wayward time machine and save his beloved wife from her latest misadventure. If only they can travel safely past the black hole…

*A Valentine's Anthology*

*The Lending Library*-a fantasy by C. L. Kraemer

Faeries try to fit into the human world when the forest where they make their home is destroyed by a mysterious enemy.

*Chasing Rainbows*-a contemporary romance by Genene Valleau

An eccentric aunt, an inventive uncle, a mother who wears poodle skirts, and a brother who wears pearls provide a hilarious backdrop for the courtship of a young woman who yearns for a "normal" family.

*The Gift*-an historical romance by Christine Young

A man and a woman on opposite sides of the Civil War get a second chance at love after one final battle returns soldiers to their war-torn homes to rebuild their lives.